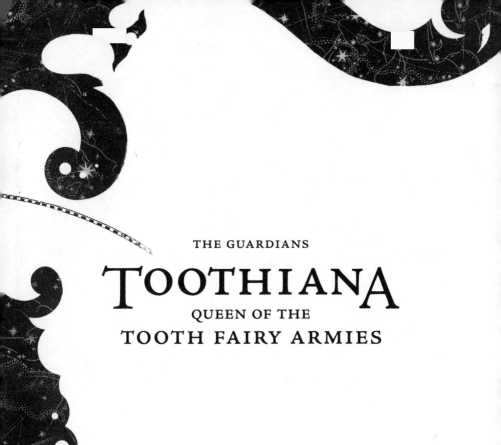

THE GUARDIANS

TOOTHIANA

QUEEN OF THE

TOOTH FAIRY ARMIES

Queen Toothiana

THE GUARDIANS

TOOTHIANA

QUEEN OF THE
TOOTH FAIRY ARMIES

WILLIAM JOYCE

Atheneum

Atheneum Books for Young Readers
NEW YORK • LONDON • TORONTO • SYDNEY • NEW DELHI

athenum

Atheneum Books for Young Readers
An imprint of Simon & Schuster Children's Publishing Division
1230 Avenue of the Americas, New York, New York 10020
For information about special discounts for bulk purchases, please contact Simon & Schuster
Special Sales at 1-866-506-1949 or business@simonandschuster.com.
The Simon & Schuster Speakers Bureau can bring authors to your live event. For more
information or to book an event, contact the Simon & Schuster Speakers Bureau at
1-866-248-3049 or visit our website at www.simonspeakers.com.
Book design by Lauren Rille
The text for this book is set in Adobe Jenson Pro.
The illustrations for this book are rendered in a combination of charcoal,
graphite, and digital media.
Manufactured in the United States of America
0812 FFG
First Edition
10 9 8 7 6 5 4 3 2 1
CIP data for this book is available from the Library of Congress.
ISBN 978-1-4424-3052-5
ISBN 978-1-4424-5461-3 (eBook)

Contents

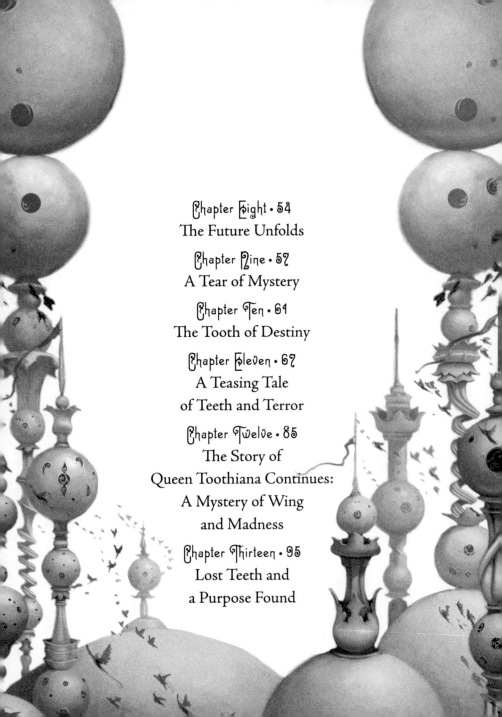

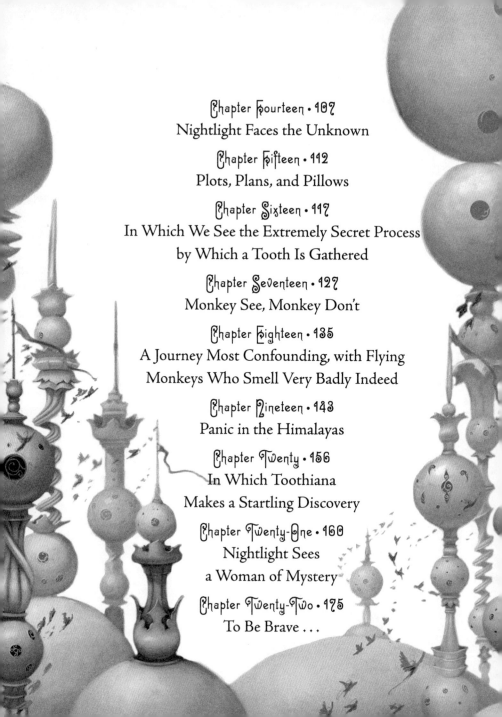

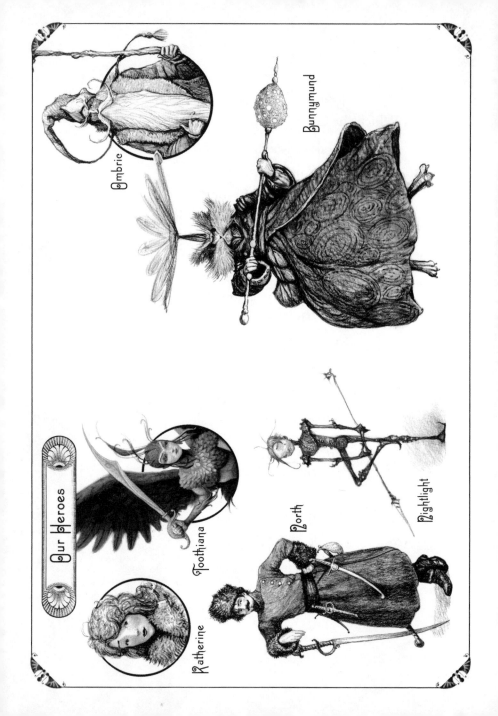

Ombric

Bunnymund

Our Heroes

Toothiana

Katherine

North

Nightlight

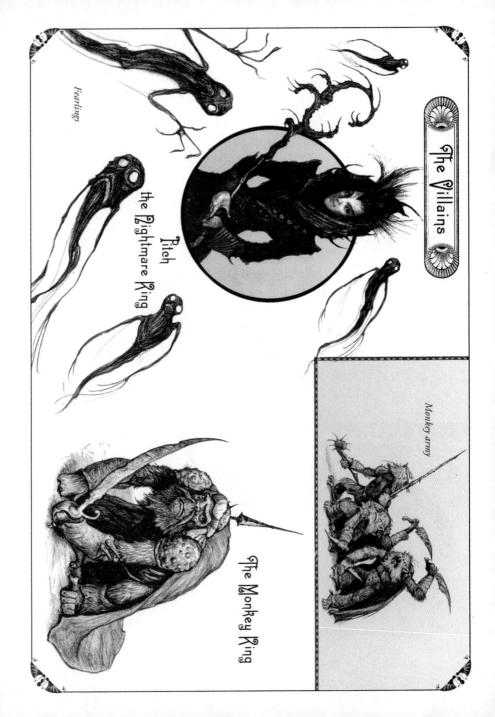

The Villains

Fearlings

Pitch the Nightmare King

Monkey army

The Monkey King

CHAPTER ONE

The Changes That Come with Peace

WILLIAM THE ABSOLUTE YOUNGEST galloped through the enchanted village of Santoff Claussen on the back of a large Warrior Egg, a gift from E. Aster Bunnymund. "I can't stop or I'll be scrambled!" he shouted over his shoulder to his friend Fog. In this new game of Warrior Egg tag, to be scrambled meant you had been caught by the opposing egg team and therefore, had lost a point.

Sascha and her brother, Petter, were in hot pursuit, riding Warrior Eggs of their own. The matchstick-thin legs of the mechanical eggs moved so fast, they were a blur.

"Comin' in for the scramble shot!" Petter warned. His long tag pole, with the egg-shaped tip, was inches away from Sascha.

"Eat my yolk," Sascha said with a triumphant laugh. She pushed a button, and suddenly, her Warrior Egg sprouted wings. She flew over the others, reaching the finish line first.

William the Absolute Youngest slowed to a trot. "Wings!" he grumbled. "They aren't even in the rules!"

"I invented them yesterday," said Sascha. "There's nothing in the rules that says you can't use 'em."

Soon Sascha was helping the youngest William construct his own set of eggbot wings. She liked the youngest William. He always tried to act older, and she appreciated his determination and spirit. Petter and Fog, feeling wild and industrious, catapulted themselves to the hollow of a tall tree where they had

erected a hideout devoted to solving ancient myster-
ies, such as: why was there such a thing as bedtime,
and what could they do to eliminate it forever?

Across the clearing, in a tree house perched high
in the branches of Big Root—the tree at the center of
the village—their friend Katherine contently watched
the children play.

The air shimmered with their happy laughter.
Many months had passed since the battle at the
Earth's core during which Pitch, the Nightmare King,
had been soundly defeated by Katherine and the
other Guardians: Ombric, the wizard; his apprentice,
Nicholas St. North; their friend Nightlight; and their
newest ally, the Pookan rabbit known as E. Aster
Bunnymund. Pitch, who had hungered for the dreams
of innocent children and longed to replace them with
nightmares, had vowed with his Fearlings to make

all the children of Earth live in terror. But since the great battle, he had not been seen or heard from, and Katherine was beginning to hope that Pitch had been vanquished forever.

As for Katherine and her battle mates, their lives were forever changed. The Man in the Moon himself had given them the title of "Guardians." They were heroes now, sworn to protect the children of not just Santoff Claussen, but the entire planet. They had defeated Pitch, and their greatest challenge at present was how to manage the peace. The "nightmare" of Pitch's reign seemed to be over.

The other children of the village now filled their days with mischief and magic. Bunnymund, who could burrow through the Earth with astonishing speed, had created a series of tunnels for them, connecting the village with his home on Easter Island and with other amazing outposts around the world, and the children had become intrepid explorers. On any given day they might journey to the African savanna to visit the lions, cheetahs, and hippopotami—Ombric had taught them a number of animal languages, so they had numerous stories to hear and tell. Many of the creatures had already heard of their amazing adventures.

The children also regularly circled through Easter Island for the latest chocolate confection Bunnymund had invented, and could still be back in time for dinner and games with Bunnymund's mechanical egg comrades. The eggs were once Bunnymund's war-riors; now they helped the children build all manner of interesting contraptions, from intricate egg-shaped puzzles where every piece was egg-shaped (a nearly impossible and frankly unexplainable feat) to egg-shaped submarines. But no matter where the children roamed or what they did to occupy their days, whenever they returned home to Santoff Claussen, it had never seemed so lovely to them.

As Katherine sat in her tree house, she put her arm around Kailash, her great Himalayan Snow Goose, and looked out on her beloved village. The forest that surrounded and protected Santoff Claussen had bloomed into a kind of eternal spring. The massive oaks and vines that had once formed an impenetrable wall against the outside world were thick with leaves of the deepest green. The huge, spear-size thorns that had once covered the vines grew pliant and blossomed with sweet-scented flowers.

Katherine loved the smell, and drew a deep breath of it. In the distance she could see Nicholas St. North walking with the beautiful, ephemeral Spirit of the Forest. She was more radiant now than ever before. Her gossamer robes were resplendent with blooms that shimmered like jewels. North was deep in conversation with her, so Katherine decided to investigate. She climbed on to Kailash's back and flew down into the clearing, just in time to see William the

Absolute Youngest try out the new wings with which he'd outfitted his Warrior Egg. He landed and trotted over to her.

"Want to race with us, Katherine?" he asked. He gave Kailash a scratch on her neck, and the goose honked a hello.

"I will later!" Katherine said, smiling. She waved to her friends and headed into the forest, realizing that it had been quite some time since any of the children had asked her to play, and an even longer time since she had accepted. In joining the world of the Guardians, she was in a strange new phase of her life—where she was neither child nor adult. As she watched the youngest William fly away with Sascha close behind him, she couldn't help but feel a bit torn.

Then she heard North's hearty laugh and, underneath that, the more musical tones of the Spirit of the Forest. Katherine hurried toward them, thinking that it was hard to believe that when North first came to Santoff Claussen with his band of outlaws, it had been with the intent to steal its treasures. The Spirit of the Forest, the village's last line of defense, had turned North's crew of cutthroats and bandits into stone statues—hideous, hunched elves. But she had spared North, for he alone among them was pure of heart.

When Katherine caught up with the Spirit and North, they were standing in that most strange and eerie part of the forest—the place where North's men stood frozen in time, like stones in a forgotten burial site. With the Spirit's help, North was bringing his bandits back to human form.

As the Spirit touched the head of each statue, North repeated the same spell, "From flesh to stone and back again. To serve with honor, your one true friend." And one by one they emerged from their frozen poses. To North's great amusement, they hadn't regained their size. They were still the same height as their stone selves—about two feet tall, with bulbous noses and high, childlike voices.

"Welcome back," North called out, slapping each of the elfin men on the back.

The men stamped their little feet and waved their little arms to get their blood flowing again, and soon the children, drawn by North's laughter, arrived. They were shocked; they often played among these small stone men, and now that they were moving—were alive, in fact—the children were most intrigued. Tall William, the first son of Old William, towered over them. Even the youngest William was overjoyed—at last he was taller than someone else.

While the children watched, the little men kneeled before North. They took on new names as they pledged to follow their former outlaw leader in a new life of goodness. Gregor of the Mighty Stink became Gregor of the Mighty Smile. Sergei the Terrible was now Sergei the Giggler, and so on.

It was an odd but auspicious moment, especially for North. He remembered his wild, unruly life as a bandit and the many dark deeds that he and these fellows had committed. He'd become a hero, a man of great learning, good humor, and some wisdom. So much had changed since that moment when he faced the temptation of the Spirit of the Forest, when he had rejected her promises of treasure and had chosen to save the children of Santoff Claussen.

North turned and looked at young Katherine. He felt the full weight of all they had been through. They had both changed. It was a change he did not fully understand, but he knew he was glad for it. For though these dwarfish fellows in front of him had once been his comrades in crime, North, in his heart, had been alone. But that was past. This was a different day. And through the friendship he now knew, he could change bad men to good and stone back to flesh.

North gently asked his old confederates to rise. They did so gladly.

Peace had indeed come.

Katherine took North's hand, and together they welcomed these baffled little men to the world of Santoff Claussen.

CHAPTER TWO

The Guardians Gather

ALTHOUGH THE CHILDREN HAD begun to refer to the battle at the Earth's core as "Pitch's Last Battle," the Guardians knew that the Nightmare King was both devious and shrewd. He could still be lurking somewhere, ready to pounce.

Nightlight, the mysterious, otherworldly boy who was Katherine's dearest friend, scoured the night sky for signs of Pitch's army. He even traveled deep into the cave where he'd been imprisoned in Pitch's icy heart for centuries, but all he found were memories of those dark times. Of Pitch and his Fearling soldiers, he could find not even an echo. Bunnymund kept his rabbit ears tuned for ominous signs while burrowing his system of tunnels, and Ombric cast his mind about for bits of dark magic that might be creeping into the world. As for North, he was being rather secretive. He kept to himself (or, rather, to his elfin friends), working quietly and diligently in the great study, deep at the center of Big Root. On what he was working, no one knew for sure, but he seemed most intense.

And every night the children clamored for Mr. Qwerty, the glowworm who had transformed himself

into a magical book. Because he had eaten every book in Ombric's library, he could tell the children any fact or story they wanted to hear. Mr.

Qwerty's pages were blank, at least until he began to read himself, and then the words and drawings would appear. But most nights the children wanted to hear one of Katherine's stories from Mr. Qwerty, for he allowed only her to write in him. But before any story was read, Katherine asked them about their dreams. Not one had had a single nightmare since the great battle.

There truly was *absolutely* no sign of Pitch. The sun seemed to shine brighter, every day seemed more beautiful, perfect, carefree. It was as if, when Pitch vanished, he took all the evil in the world with him.

Even so, the Guardians knew that wickedness of Pitch's magnitude did not surrender easily. They met together every day, never at an appointed time, but when it somehow seemed right. Their bond of friendship was so strong that it now connected them in heart and mind. Each could often sense what the others felt, and when it felt like the time to gather, they would just somehow *know*. They would drop what they were doing and go to Big Root, where, with cups of tea, they'd discuss any possible signs of Pitch's return.

On this particular day Nightlight hadn't far to travel. The night before, he'd stayed in Big Root's tree-top all through the night, having searched every corner of the globe at dusk and found nothing alarming. Though he could fly forever, and never slept, his habit was to watch over Katherine and Kailash. More and more often the girl and her goose slept in their nest-like tree house, and so Nightlight would join them and guard them till morning.

Among the Guardians, his and Katherine's bond was the greatest. It hovered in a lovely realm that went past words and descriptions. The two never tired of the other's company and felt a pang of sadness when apart. But even that ache was somehow exquisite, for they knew that they would never be separated for long. Nightlight would never let that be so. Nor would Katherine. Time and time again they had managed a way to find each other, no matter how desperate the circumstances.

So Nightlight felt most perfectly at peace when watching over Katherine as she slept. Sleep was a mystery to him, and in some ways, so was dreaming. It worried him, in fact. Katherine was there but not entirely. Her mind traveled to Dreamlands where he could not follow.

In his childish way, he longed to go with her. And on this night, he had found a way to trespass into the unknown realm of her sleeping mind.

As he'd sat beside Katherine and her goose as they slept, he'd looked up to the Moon. His friend was full and bright. In these peaceful times the playful moonbeams came to him less often than before. There were no worries or urgent messages from the Man in the Moon, and so Nightlight could now enjoy the silent beauty of his benefactor. But a glint of something on Katherine's cheek had reflected the Moon's glow. Nightlight leaned in closely.

It was a tear. A tear? This confounded him. What was there in her dream that would make Katherine cry? He knew about the power of tears. It was from tears that his diamond dagger was forged. But those tears were from wakeful times. He had never touched a Dream Tear. But before he could think better of it, he reached down and gently plucked it up.

Dream Tears are very powerful, and when

Nightlight first tried to look into it, he was nearly knocked from the tree. He caught his balance and carefully looked at the small drop. Inside was Katherine's dream. And what he saw there seared his soul. For the first time in all his strange and dazzling life, Nightlight felt a deep, unsettling fear.

There, haunting her dreams, he had seen Pitch.

Nightlight and the Dream Tear

CHAPTER THREE

Nightlight Must Lie

Now, as Nightlight shimmered his way into the waiting room of Big Root, he was the last to arrive. He kept his distance, perching high on one of the bookcases. Ombric and Bunnymund were poring over a map of the lost city of Atlantis. Katherine spied Nightlight and could tell immediately that something was troubling him.

North began regaling Ombric with the news about his band of brigands and their new lives as elfin helpers.

Ombric's left eyebrow rose high; he was clearly

amused. "Well done, Nicholas. I see great things in store for your little men," he said.

Though neither man would say out loud how they felt, Katherine could tell Ombric was immensely proud of his apprentice, and North took great pleasure in Ombric's approval. She felt a surge of happiness for the both of them.

Bunnymund's ears twitched. *These humans and their emotions,* he thought. *They are so odd. They are more interested in feelings than chocolate!*

"Any sign of Pitch today?" he asked politely but pointedly.

North shook his head. "The old grump hasn't grumbled."

"None of the children have had bad dreams," reported Katherine.

Nightlight didn't respond. He knew otherwise.

Or, at least, he thought he did.

Bunnymund then answered his own question. "And nothing in my tunnels—nothing evil or unchocolatey or anti-egg anywhere."

Ombric stroked his beard. "Perhaps the children are correct," he mused, "and the battle at the Earth's core truly was Pitch's *last* battle."

North pondered. "Can that really be?"

Katherine turned to Nightlight. She generally knew what he was thinking, but today she couldn't read him. "Nightlight," she prompted, "have you seen anything?"

He shifted on his perch. His brow furrowed, but he shook his head.

It was the first time Nightlight had ever lied.

CHAPTER FOUR

A Celebration, an Insect Symphony, and a Troublesome Feeling

I

T'S NOW BEEN EIGHT months since we last saw
Pitch. I think before we declare victory, it would be
best to consult with the Man in the Moon," Ombric
said. "And that means a journey to—"

"The Lunar Lamadary!" Bunnymund and North
said together. The Lamadary sat on the highest peak
of one of the highest Himalayan mountains, and it
was there where North had first met both the Lunar
Lamas and the Man in the Moon.

North was ready to leave that minute. It was a
great chance to meet again with the Yeti warriors

who defended the city. They had been quite help-ful when North had been learning the secrets of the magic sword the Man in the Moon had bestowed upon him. The sword was a relic from the Golden Age, and there were five of these relics in total. Bunnymund had one as well—the egg-shaped tip to his staff. The Man in the Moon had said that if all five were gathered together, they would create a force powerful enough to defeat Pitch forever. But peace seemed to be at hand. With any luck, the Guardians would have no need for more relics. But North *had* been wondering how he would keep his warrior skills sharp, or if he even should. With the Yetis, he'd again have able competitors with whom to practice his swordmanship.

Ombric turned to Bunnymund. He didn't even have to ask about making a tunnel, because next to making chocolate eggs, digging tunnels was the Pooka's favorite pastime.

"One tunnel coming up," Bunnymund said. "It'll be ready in twenty-seven half yolks—that's one day in your human time."

"Outstanding," Ombric said with a nod. "We'll take the whole village—everyone is welcome!" he added. "It'll be a grand adventure. We'll plan a celebration tomorrow evening to see us off!"

Katherine clapped her hands together in excitement. *Kailash will be so happy to see the other Great Snow Geese,* she thought. She'd wondered if her goose ever missed the flock of massive birds that nested in the Lunar Lamas' mountain peak.

But her excitement was tempered by her unease about Nightlight. She glanced at him, but he would not return her gaze. Instead, with his amazing speed, he shot out the window and into the clear, blue sky. But he did not seem bright, Katherine noted, and her unease grew.

The next day found Santoff Claussen full of preparations for the trip and for a celebratory dinner. The eggbots whipped up frothy confections, and the ants, centipedes, and beetles tidied Big Root while glowworms set up tables in the clearing—tables that would be heaped with delicious foods. Not to be left out, squirrels made teetering piles of nuts, birds filled their feeders with seed, and mouthwatering smells came from every nook and cranny of the village.

That evening the children led a parade of humans; elvish men; insects, birds; their great bear; the djinni; North's wonder horse, Petrov; and one very tall Pooka to the well-decorated clearing.

The Moon was so luminous that the villagers were sure they could see the Man in the Moon himself smiling down on them. The Lunar Moths glowed, and Ombric's many owls hooted softly. Soon the children were jumping onto the backs of the village reindeer and racing them across the evening sky while Katherine and Kailash flew alongside. Fireflies circled their heads, making halos of green-tinged light.

Down below, North's elves ate plate after plate of jam roly-poly, noodle pudding, and sweet potato schnitzel, topping off the meal with elderberry pie and Bunnymund's newest chocolates—a delectable blend of Aztec cacao and purple plum—all the while asking North to describe the meals prepared by the Yetis (accomplished chefs all) at the Lunar Lamadary. It seemed that being turned to stone and back again was a hungry business.

Even the crickets came out into the moonlight to play a sort of insect symphony to the delight of everyone.

Finally, when all the games had been played, the food eaten, and the songs sung, the village of Santoff Claussen settled down to sleep.

Up in her tree house, however, Katherine lay awake. Nightlight had been the only one who had not joined the party that night. And it bothered her. As did something else: Ever since the last battle, Katherine found that in quiet moments like this, her mind often drifted back to Pitch and his daughter—the little girl he had fathered and loved before he'd been consumed by evil. In the final moments of their battle, Katherine had shown Pitch a locket—a locket that held his daughter's picture. She could not stop thinking about the anguished look on Pitch's face, or her own longing to be loved as deeply as Pitch's daughter had been loved by her father.

Does that feeling only happen between parent and child, a father and a daughter? Katherine wondered. She had lost her own parents when she was just a baby. It was true that here in Santoff Claussen, many people loved her and cared for her. Ombric and North were like a father and a brother to her. But that wasn't the same as a *real* family, was it? She couldn't help wondering whether anyone would feel that same anguish she'd seen in Pitch's eyes if she were lost to them.

And there was Nightlight. She sensed his current melancholy.

He's never had a parent, she thought, *and he had seemed happy enough.* But now something was wrong. She would find out what it was. She would make him happy once more. And then maybe she'd be happy too.

That thought brought comfort to the gray-eyed girl, and soon, like everyone else in the village, she was asleep.

But a strange wind blew through Santoff Claussen. It caused the limbs of Katherine's tree house to gently sway. If Katherine had awakened, she'd have felt uneasy, as though she were being watched by a force nearly as ancient as Pitch. Whose motives and deeds would change everything. If Katherine just opened her eyes, she'd have seen what was in store.

CHAPTER FIVE

An Amazing Journey
to the Top of the World

THE NEXT MORNING THE whole village gathered at the entrance of Bunnymund's latest digging extravaganza: a tunnel that would take them to the Lunar Lamadary.

With great fanfare, Bunnymund swung open the tunnel's egg-shaped door and stepped into the first car of the extraordinary locomotive that would speed them on their way. Trains were still not yet invented (Bunnymund would secretly help the credited inventors some decades later), so the machine and its technology were still a source of considerable amazement for the people of Santoff Claussen. Like the tunnel he had created, Bunnymund's railway train was also egg-shaped, as was every knob, door, window, and light fixture. It was easy to tell he was quite proud of his creation.

Ombric, North, Katherine, and Kailash, along with North's elfin comrades, the children, and their parents, scrambled on board. Bunnymund was twist-ing and turning the myriad of egg-shaped controls.

The Spirit of the Forest waved her shimmering veils at them as Bunnymund started the engine.

"Aren't you coming?" Katherine called out, hang-ing from a window.

The Spirit of the Forest shook her head, the jewels in her hair casting a glistening, rainbowlike glow around her. "I'm a creature of the forest, and in the forest I will stay. Petrov, Bear, the eggbots, the djinni, and I will watch over the village while you are away." The gardens of flowers around her seemed to be nodding in agreement as the villagers waved good-bye with calls of "See you soon" and "We'll miss you."

As soon as the train began to move, Sascha turned to Katherine excitedly. "Tell us again about the Lunar Lamas!" she said.

"And the Yetis!" her brother Petter added.

But Katherine was distracted. Nightlight hadn't gotten on board. In fact, she hadn't seen him since yesterday afternoon. She looked out the window as the train began to descend into the tunnel. *Where is he?* Then, as the last car heaved downward, she glimpsed him swooping into a window at the back of the train. She felt instantly better.

"Please, will you tell us of the Yetis?" the smallest William begged, pulling on Katherine's shirtsleeve. She turned to him with a smile now that she knew Nightlight was at least on board. She searched through the pages of Mr. Qwerty until she came to the drawing she had made of the Grand High Lama. His round face seemed to beam at them. "The Lamas, remember, are holy men," Katherine told them, "even older than Ombric! They've devoted their whole lives to studying the Man in the Moon. They know all about Nightlight and how he used to protect the little Man in the Moon in the Golden Age before Pitch—"

Katherine cut herself off. She did *not* want to think about Pitch right now.

"The Lamas live in a palace . . . ," Sascha prompted.

"Not a palace, really. But a fantastic place called a Lamadary." Katherine turned the page, revealing the Lamas' home, glowing as if with moonlight. "There's nowhere else on Earth closer to the Moon than the Lunar Lamadary."

"Now tell us about the Yetis," Petter begged.

"The Yetis—oh, they are magnificent creatures . . . ," Katherine said, but her voice began to trail off. "They helped us defeat Pitch...."

"I can't wait to see it all with my own eyes," Sascha said dreamily. "Especially the Man in the Moon."

"And mountains so high, we'll be above the clouds," Fog added.

The children began chattering among themselves about the adventures to come, not noticing that Katherine had grown quiet.

She rose from her seat. She felt uneasy again, and the children's company didn't suit her right now. She didn't really know where she wanted to be—with the children or with North and the other grown-ups. Even Kailash didn't comfort her. She was betwixt and between. She started toward the back of the train. The only company she desired right now was Nightlight's.

CHAPTER SIX

The Chicken or the Egg: A Puzzle

WHILE THE CHILDREN WERE anticipating their first trip to the Himalayas, Ombric and Bunnymund were in a deep debate about which came first, the chicken or the egg. Ombric believed it was the chicken. Bunnymund, not surprisingly, believed it was the egg. But the Pooka had to admit that he could not answer the question definitively.

"Eggs are the most perfect shape in the universe," he argued. "It's logical that the egg would come first and the chicken would follow."

"But where did the first egg come from, if the

chicken did not exist?" Ombric asked.

"Where did the chicken come from," Bunnymund pointed out, "if not from the egg?"

Privately, each one believed he had won the argument, but publicly, the wizard deferred to the Pooka. Bunnymund was the only creature alive who was both older and wiser than Ombric. In fact, when Ombric had been a young boy in Atlantis and had first experimented with his magic, it had been Bunnymund who had saved him from a most tragic end.

Ombric had learned so much since he'd become reacquainted with the Pooka. He felt almost like a student again. But perhaps, he thought, he had something to teach E. Aster.

"Have you ever met the Lunar Lamas?" Ombric asked, eager to fill him in on their strange ways.

"Yes and no," Bunnymund replied mysteriously.

"It *was* rather difficult getting that mountain in place before their ship crashed to Earth back, oh, before the beginning of *your* recorded time. So we have what you might call 'a history,' but does anyone *really* know anyone? I mean to say, I've met them, I've talked to them, I've read their minds and they've read mine, but do I know what they'll say or do next at any given moment or what underwear they wear on Tuesdays and why? Do I? Do I *really* know?"

Ombric blinked and tried to take in all that information. It was an answer of sorts. "Indeed," he said at last. "Um . . . yes . . . well . . . all right . . . That must be how they knew to point us in your direction when we sought the relic." He glanced up at the sumptuously bejeweled egg that adorned the top of Bunnymund's staff and raised an eyebrow. "They would tell us only—"

"That I was mysterious and preferred to remain unknown," Bunnymund finished for him, steering the train around a graceful, oval curve. "True. Absolutely true. Etched in stone, so to speak. At least until I made the curiously rewarding acquaintance of you and your fellows. Most unexpected. Utterly surprising. And, as you say, 'a hoot.'" Bunnymund had developed a genuine pleasure in using the new expressions he heard in the company of what he called "Earthlings."

Ombric smiled at the fellow. "I like you too, Bunnymund."

The rabbit's ears twitched. Such obvious statements of Earthling sentiments never failed to baffle him. Yet, while the Pooka would never admit it, Ombric could tell that he was beginning to actually enjoy the company of humans—in small doses, anyway.

◆ ◆ ◆

As they neared the Himalayas, Katherine combed through car after car of chattering villagers and elves, looking for Nightlight. North's elves were busily working on what looked like a drawing or plans for something. They cheerfully covered their pages from her view. She decided not to pry, for she rather liked these funny little men. But more to the point, she was on a mission to find Nightlight.

Then, as it always happened, she suddenly knew that it was time for her to meet with the other Guardians, and she could sense that Nightlight was there with them. She followed this feeling as it led her to the train's front car, or as Bunnymund referred to it, the Eggomotive.

They were all there: North in the back by the door, Ombric and Bunnymund tinkering excitedly with the controls. And out the front window she could see Nightlight, sitting face forward in front of the engine's smokestack. He did not turn around though she knew he could feel her presence. His hair was blowing wildly as the train blasted ahead. The sound of the train was loud, but it was pleasing, like ten thousand whisks scrambling countless eggs. *Perhaps Nightlight misses all the excitement of battle,* Katherine thought, watching him lean forward into the air rushing past.

She wondered if North did as well. He was humming to himself, a faraway look on his face. Something was now different about the young wizard. He was still always ready to leap into action, still loved conjuring up new toys for the children. (Just that morning he'd brought the youngest William a funny sort of toy—a round biscuit-shaped piece of wood with a string attached to its middle. When jerked, it would go up and down almost magically. North called it a "yo-yo-ho.") And he still continued to tease Bunnymund, whom he insisted on calling "Bunny Man" no matter how many times the Pooka corrected him. Nevertheless, Katherine sensed a change, a change she couldn't quite put her finger on. In those moments when he thought no one was looking, North had become quieter, more contemplative.

And yet he didn't seem sad or melancholy or lonely like Nightlight did. His face was alive with excitement. *What is he up to?* she wondered, hoping that, when he was ready, he would tell her about it. If only she could be sure that Nightlight would be so forthcoming. *All this change is so unsettling. Peace is harder than I thought it would be.*

North, sensing her presence, grinned and brushed

a lock of hair from her forehead. "Ready to see the Man in the Moon again?"

Katherine gave him an impish smile, and nodded yes. She could feel the train beginning to climb upward. The engine strained to pull the egg-shaped cars and their festive cargo up toward the Himalayan mountain peak. They were nearly there.

CHAPTER SEVEN

In Which the Man in the Moon Greets the Guardians with a Fair Amount of Fanfare

THE GUARDIANS EXCHANGED LOOKS full of anticipation. Even Bunnymund, who considered anything nonchocolate or egg-related to be of little importance, looked forward to sharing the news that they believed Pitch had been vanquished.

For the last few minutes of the journey the train was traveling completely vertical—Katherine had to hang on to North or she'd slide out the door. Then the first car popped out of the tunnel into the clear, perfect light of the highest place on Earth. A new egg-shaped Eggomotive station was in place, and the train came to rest at the outskirts of the Lunar Lamadary.

The holy men now waited on the platform in their silver slippers and billowing silk-spun robes. They bowed deeply at the sight of Nightlight, who hopped lightly off the engine. Having once been the protector of the Man in the Moon, Nightlight always received their greatest reverence. Their Moon-like faces, normally inscrutable, resonated joy at his arrival. And this seemed to brighten Nightlight's mood as well. But he was still distant with Katherine.

Old William and his sons, along with all the other parents and children, gaped in wonder at the sight of the Lamas' headquarters and the cool, serene, creamy glow of its moonstone and opal mosaics. Sascha nearly tumbled out of the train's window in her effort to see the Lamadary's famous tower, which was also an airship. Even Mr. Qwerty, his pages fluttering, hurried toward the train's doors to get a closer look.

Gongs rang out. Bells—hundreds of them—chimed in the wind. Yaloo, the leader of the Yetis, stood with the Snow Geese at the edge of the platform, and blew a silver horn forged from ancient meteors, as the Snow Geese honked a warm "hello" at the sight of Kailash and Katherine.

As the welcoming reverberations quieted, Ombric stepped onto the platform. "Greetings, my good friends," he addressed the gathering. "We've come to speak to the Man in the Moon . . . and to report what we think is historic news."

The old man was clearly eager to see the Man in the Moon and share their findings, but there were the curiously slow habits of the Lamas to consider. They never did anything quickly and were usually very, very, very talkative. And yet, surprisingly, it seemed that the Lamas were just as eager to proceed. It was highly unusual for them to rush for any reason, but today they whisked everyone off the train and directly toward the Lamadary's courtyard.

The Yetis lined the outer edges of the courtyard as the Lamas led everyone else to the huge gong at its very center.

The children could barely contain their excitement. The Man in the Moon was about to be summoned!

The Grand High Lama glided forward. He smiled serenely, then, with almost shocking suddenness, he struck the great gong with his gilded scepter. The sound was sweet and strong. It grew and echoed throughout the temple, then throughout the mountains around them until it sounded as though the whole Earth was humming a gentle "hello" to the heavens.

The gong itself began to shimmer, shifting from a solid metal to a clear, glasslike substance. And as the children pointed in astonishment, the Moon began to appear in the milky light at the gong's center, swelling in size until a face emerged from the craters—the kindest, gentlest face anyone could imagine.

The Lamas bowed, as did the five Guardians and everyone else in the courtyard. As they stood up, Nightlight and the friendly moonbeam that lived in the diamond tip of his staff blinked a greeting. North raised his sword in salute and noticed that it had begun to glow. So did the egg on the tip of Bunnymund's staff. Katherine held her dagger aloft exactly as she had when she had vowed to battle Pitch so many months ago, and Ombric simply placed the palms of his hands together and lowered his head even farther in greeting.

The Man in the Moon

"Tsar Lunar," he said in a reverent tone, "we've scoured the Earth for Pitch and found no trace of him. Can you tell us, has he truly been defeated?"

The image on the gong flickered and waned like moonlight on a cloudy night. The Man in the Moon's voice was so deep, it almost seemed like a heartbeat. "My valiant friends," he said. "Each night I send thousands of moonbeams down to Earth, and each night they return clear and untarnished by Pitch's dark ways." As he spoke, a wide smile spread across his face.

Cheers rung out throughout the Lamadary.

"It appears

the world is on the cusp of a new Golden Age," he continued, "a Golden Age on Earth. And it is you, my Guardians, who must guide its creation. It is a task of great daring imagination and thoughtful dreaming."

Everyone's eyes turned to Ombric, Katherine, Bunnymund, North, and Nightlight. One old, one young, one from another world, one who overcame a most disreputable beginning, and one a spirit of light. Such a group *could* bring about a Golden Age. But who would lead this historic endeavor?

To everyone's surprise, it was North who stepped forward. "I have a plan," he said.

He sheathed his sword and raised his other hand, opening his palm to reveal a small paper box covered with minute drawings and plans. Katherine recognized it. *It's what the elves were working on!*

"This was a gift, one that I now pass on," North began, stealing a glance at Katherine and then turning back to the Man in the Moon. "A dream for the new Golden Age."

CHAPTER EIGHT

The Future Unfolds

WITH THAT, NORTH CLOSED his eyes for a moment, recalling Ombric's first lesson: The power of magic lies in believing. He began to chant, "I believe, I believe."

Ombric, Katherine, and even Bunnymund joined him, quickly followed by the entire courtyard, and the box in North's hand unfolded into a vast origami wonder.

A magical city seemed to grow out of North's palm. Ombric's eyebrows raised. North was becoming something more powerful than a warrior *or* a wizard. Ombric could sense it.

North tipped his head toward Katherine, whose eyes were shining—this was the dream *she* had given him when all seemed lost during one of the first great battles with Pitch! A dream in which North was a powerful figure of mirth, mystery, and magic, who lived in a city surrounded by snow.

Katherine nodded back encouragingly, and so North started.

"I have a plan for building new centers of magic and learning," North explained. "One village like Santoff Claussen is not enough, and to expand it would be to change it. What we need instead are more places where all those with kind hearts and inquiring minds—inventors, scientists, artists, and visionaries—will be welcomed and encouraged. Where children will always be safe and protected and grow to become their finest selves."

The paper city hovered in the air just above North's palm. There was a great castlelike structure in its center, surrounded by workshops and cottages. A tiny Nicholas St. North could be seen striding through the village center, with his elves and Petrov, his horse, by his side. And a herd of mighty reindeer. The Yetis too were there.

North bowed his head and waited for the Man in the Moon's response. He'd thought he might feel anxious at this moment; instead, he felt peaceful—more peaceful than he could ever remember feeling. He had shared the truest dream of his heart.

The Man in the Moon gazed down at North. He didn't need to say anything. His luminous smile said all that needed saying.

CHAPTER NINE

A Tear of Mystery

WITH ALL THE HURLY-BURLY and hubbub surrounding this new Golden Age and the city North would build, Katherine found herself lost in the shuffle. The adult Guardians were in a frenzy of excitement, talking heatedly among themselves. She didn't mind, really. It made her happy to see North and Ombric in deep discussions again; it was like old times. And watching Bunnymund interject ideas was always amusing. He was enthusiastic as long as the plans involved chocolate or eggs. As the discussions went on, she realized they'd made a slight breakthrough. Bunnymund was now willing to broaden his interest to other types of candies. "Anything that is sweet has great philosophical and curative powers, and as such, could be key to this new Golden Age!" he pronounced with his usual droll pookery.

The villagers of Santoff Claussen were also happily speculating about new innovations and technologies. The children, especially, were caught up in the commotion. Sascha and the youngest William came up to Katherine. "What do you think this all means?" Sascha asked.

Katherine thought a moment, then answered, "It means that there'll be amazing new things to invent and build and see and do." Sascha's and William's eyes grew bright as they tried to imagine what this future would be like.

As if reading their minds, Katherine added, "Everything will be . . . different."

Before they could ask her to explain, she caught a glimpse of Nightlight up on the highest tower of the Lamadary, and she hurried after him. All his dodging about had her increasingly worried. She could not *feel* his friendship. She could feel nothing from him at all.

The steps to the bell tower were steeper than she'd expected and proved hard to climb. North's compass, which she hadn't taken off since he'd given it to her all those long months ago, was swinging back and forth, thunking against her chest in a most annoying way. But she didn't stop to remove it; she just climbed on.

I hope Nightlight hasn't flown off, she thought, trying to see around a corner as she neared the top steps. She began climbing much more quietly. Through an arched window, she could see him on the other side, perched on the ledge. His back was to her, but she could see that his head hung low, almost to his knees. The light from the diamond point of his staff was dim. And for the first time in days, she could sense his feelings; his feelings were sad. Very sad.

She'd never known Nightlight to be sad! She crept closer still, until she could see that he was holding something. Carefully, carefully, without making a sound, she balanced herself out onto the ledge right next to him. In his hand he held something. She leaned forward even closer. It was a tear. A single tear.

Nightlight suddenly realized she was there. He jumped to his feet with an abruptness that startled her. She teetered for a moment, windmilling her arms for balance.

In a terrible instant, she fell from the ledge.

CHAPTER TEN

The Tooth of Destiny

FALLING TO YOUR DEATH is a strange and unsettling sensation. Your mind becomes very sharp. Time seems to slow down. You are able to think an incredible number of thoughts at astonishing speed. These were Katherine's thoughts for the three and a half seconds before she came in contact with the cobblestone courtyard of the Lunar Lamadary:

Oh oh oh oh! Falling! I'm falling!!! FAAALL-LING!!!!! Not good!! Maybe I'm not falling. Please-pleasepleasepleeeeese say I'm not falling. WRONG!!! FALLING!!! Falling FAST!!!! FastFastFastFast . . . Slow

DOWN . . . *Can't CAN'T . . . Not good . . . Okay . . . think . . . How do I stop? I DON'T KNOW!!!!! Okay, okay, okay . . . I HATE GRAVITY . . . GRAVITY!!! HATE!!! HATE!!! HATE GRAVITY!!!!! Hairs in my mouth . . . My hair . . . Yuck . . . Spit . . . Okay . . . Hairs out of mouth . . . FALLING!!!! STILL FALLING!!!!! A tear? Why was Nightlight holding a tear? . . . Sad . . . real sad . . . SAD!!! SAD THAT I'M FALLING . . . Where is everybody? . . . There are flying people everywhere in this place. . . . FLYING PEOPLE HELP NOW!!!! RIGHT NOW!!! I'M YOUR FALLING FRIEND HERE . . . FALLING FAAAAAST . . . I MEAN IT!!! Where are all my magic flying friends? . . . Hellooo . . . falling Katherine . . . could USE A HAND . . . NOW!!!! Now NOW NOW NOWWWWWW!!! Is that Nightlight? . . . Can't tell . . . OH NO TURNING FALLING FAST DOWN GROUND COMING NOT GOOD*

NOT GOOD NOT GOOD . . . GROUND . . .
Happy thoughts . . . kittens . . . chocolate . . . baby mice . . .
family . . . friends . . . family . . . favorite pillow . . . friends . . .
favorite pillow . . . North . . . Ombric . . . MOON . . . Bun-
nymund . . . North . . . Nightlight . . . NIGHTLIGHT!
NIGHTLIGHT! NIGHTLIGHT! SAVE ME!!!

Then, as she screamed and thought her life was ended, her chin came into contact with the cobblestone courtyard, and she suddenly stopped falling. Nightlight had caught her left foot.

He was floating.

So now Katherine was as well. Or almost. Her chin nicked against a cobblestone, but the rest of her was held aloft. For a moment she was speechless. And when she did try to talk, she found it difficult. There was something small and hard in her mouth, like a pebble. She instinctively spit it onto the ground

beneath her. Out bounced not a pebble but . . . a tooth!
Her tooth. Her last baby tooth.

And before she could even say "ouch," chimes
rang out as every bell in the Lunar Lamadary began
to toll. And suddenly the entire troop of Lamas and
the Yetis were surrounding her and Nightlight. They
were chanting and bowing and bowing and chanting.

"Most auspicious," said the Grand High Lama.

"A tooth . . . ," said another.

". . . of a child . . . ," said a taller one.

". . . of a Guardian child . . . ," said a roundish one.

"A lost tooth . . . ," said the shortest one.

"The TOOTH . . . ," said the Grand High Lama
with a touch of awe, ". . . OF DESTINY!"

Then they started up bowing and chanting again.
Nightlight gently lowered Katherine to the ground,
then helped her up, and together they stood, baffled.

Katherine, Nightlight,
and the bond of the lost tooth

But even more baffling to Katherine was the strange look on Nightlight's face. He was trying to hide it. But he didn't know how. He was so confused by all that was happening and how close he'd come to losing Katherine. She was growing up. Nightlight's worst fear—his *only* fear—was coming true. He did not understand growing up. He did not know if he could grow up. And he did not want to be left behind if she did. But he had saved her, and as she placed her finger in the empty spot where her tooth had been, he knew that everything would be different. But there was only one thing he could do—smile at the gap in her grin.

CHAPTER ELEVEN

A Teasing Tale
of Teeth and Terror

IT TOOK NORTH, OMBRIC, and Bunnymund a few minutes to shift gears from planning a new Golden Age to understanding the importance of Katherine's lost tooth.

They had been gathered in conference in the Lamadary library when the Lunar Lamas filled the chamber, presenting Katherine and her tooth with great pomp and circumstance, proclaiming it "a lost tooth of destiny."

Bunnymund was particularly vexed by the interruption. "If Katherine is unharmed, then what is all this fuss about a tooth?" he asked, one ear twitching. "It isn't actually lost. She holds it in her hand, and now she'll grow another one. It's all very natural and, frankly, rather ordinary. It's not like she lost a chocolate truffled egg or anything."

Then the Grand High Lama described Katherine's fall and hairbreadth rescue.

Bunnymund felt a twinge of shame. He didn't mean to discount Katherine's terrifying accident. But still, a tooth was just a tooth.

The Lamas pressed on.

"We Lamas do not have baby teeth to lose," explained the Grand High Lama.

"At least, not since before recorded time," added the shortest Lama.

"And we've never had a child at the Lamadary . . . ," said the tallest Lama.

"...who's lost a child's tooth," said the least ancient Lama.

"So we've never been visited by Her Most Royal Highness," stressed the Grand High Lama.

The mention of a "Most Royal Highness" piqued everyone else's collective interest.

"Her Most Royal Highness who?" asked North, certain that if this personage dwelled on this continent, he'd likely stolen something from her in his crime-filled younger years. Ombric leaned forward, also eager to hear the Lamas' answer.

The Grand High Lama actually looked shocked by their ignorance. "Why, Her Most Royal Highness, Queen Toothiana, gatherer and protector of children's lost teeth!"

Well, that raised eyebrows from every one of them. Everyone except Bunnymund.

"Oh, her," he said dismissively. "She dislikes chocolate. She claims it's bad for children's teeth." He sniffed. "For confectionery's sake, they all fall out, anyway."

But Ombric, North, and especially Katherine wanted to know more. "I've read something about her once, I believe—" Ombric was saying, trying to remember, when a quiet cough interrupted him.

They all turned. Mr. Qwerty was standing on one of the library's Moon-shaped tables.

"Mr. Qwerty knows something," Katherine said.

The bookworm bowed and told them, "The story of the Queen of Toothiana lies in volume six of *Curious Unexplainables of the East.*"

"Of course! I should have remembered that myself," Ombric said, nodding. "Mr. Qwerty, please enlighten us."

The Guardians sat around the table while Mr. Qwerty began his tale.

"To know the story of Queen Toothiana," he said, "you must first hear the tale of the maharaja, his slave Haroom, and the Sisters of Flight."

"Sisters of Flight?" North interrupted.

"Sisters of Flight," Mr. Qwerty repeated patiently. The image of a beautiful winged woman appeared on one of Mr. Qwerty's pages. She was human-size, with long, willowy arms and legs and a heart-shaped face. But her wings were magnificent, and she held a bow and arrow of extraordinary design.

"Can she really fly?" Katherine asked in awe.

"Please, allow me to tell

the tale," Mr. Qwerty said. "The Sisters of Flight were an immortal race of winged women who ruled the city of Punjam Hy Loo, which sits atop the steepest mountain in the mysterious lands of the Farthest East. An army of noble elephants stood guard at the base of the mountain. No humans were allowed to enter, for the mountain's jungle was a haven for the beasts of the wild—a place where they could be safe from men and their foolishness."

Bunnymund's nose twitched. "Men are certainly full of *that*," he agreed.

North's nostrils flared, ready to argue with the Pooka, but Mr. Qwerty quietly continued.

"Toothiana's father was a human by the name of Haroom. He had been sold at birth into slavery as a companion for a young Indian maharaja. Despite being slave and master, the maharaja and Haroom

Haroom,
the slave with the heart of a prince

became great friends. But the maharaja was a silly, vain boy who had his every wish and whim granted. Yet this did not make him happy, for he always wanted more.

"Haroom, who had nothing, wanted nothing and so was very content. Secretly, the maharaja admired his friend for this. For his part, Haroom admired the maharaja for knowing what he wanted—and getting it."

Katherine scooted closer to Mr. Qwerty, peeking at the images of Haroom and the maharaja that now appeared on his pages. *How had a slave become the father of a queen?*

Mr. Qwerty straightened his pages and continued. "The maharaja loved to hunt and slay all the animals of the wild, and Haroom, who never tired of watching the powerful elegance of wild creatures such as tigers and snow leopards, was an excellent tracker. But he hated to see the animals killed, so when that moment came, he always looked away. As a slave, he could do nothing to stop his master. And so, with Haroom tracking, the maharaja killed one of every beast in his kingdom, lining the palace walls with their heads as trophies. But the one animal the maharaja coveted most continued to elude him.

"In the mountain land ruled by the Sisters of Flight, there dwelled one creature that no slave, man, or ruler had ever seen: the flying elephant of Punjam Hy Loo."

Katherine was impressed. "A flying *elephant?*"

Mr. Qwerty nodded. "Indeed, a flying elephant. The maharaja was determined to do anything to have one for his collection, but every time he tried to force his way up the mountain, the elephant army at its base turned him back. He realized that he must find another way to reach Punjam Hy Loo.

"In those ancient times no man had yet discovered the mystery of flight. But after demanding advice from his wizards and soothsayers, the maharaja learned a secret: Children can fly when they dream, and when the Moon shines brightly, their dreams can become so vivid that some of them come true. Sometimes the children remember, but mostly they do not. That is why children sometimes wake up in their parents' beds without knowing how they got there—they flew!

"The wizards told the maharaja a second secret." At this, Mr. Qwerty lowered his voice, and all the Guardians leaned closer. "The memory of everything that happens to a child is stored in that child's baby teeth.

"And so the maharaja's wizards gave him an idea: fashion a craft of the lost teeth of children and command it to remember how to fly. The maharaja sent out a decree throughout his kingdom, stating that whenever a child lost a tooth, it must be brought to his palace. His subjects happily complied, and it was not long before he had assembled a craft unlike any other the world had ever known."

Once again an image formed on one of Mr. Qwerty's blank pages. It was of a ship of gleaming white, fashioned from thousands of interlocking teeth. It had wings on each side of an oval gondola. The inside was lined with sumptuous carpets and intricately patterned pillows. And a single lamp hung from a mast to light the way.

"Meanwhile, the maharaja ordered Haroom to make an archer's bow of purest gold and one single ruby-tipped arrow. When the weapon was finished, the maharaja ordered Haroom to join him aboard the craft. Then he said these magic words:

"'Remember,
remember,
the moonlit flights
of magic nights.'

The maharaja's
Flying Tooth Mobile

"And just as the royal wizards had promised, the craft flew silently through the sky, over the jungle, and past the elephants who guarded Punjam Hy Loo.

"They descended from the clouds and flew into the still-sleeping city. In the misty light of dawn, the maharaja could hardly tell where the jungle ended and the city began. But Haroom, used to seeking out tracks, spotted some he had never seen before— tracks that could only belong to the flying elephant, for although they looked similar to a normal elephant's, his keen eye saw one addition: an extra digit pointing backward, like that of a bird.

"It did not take long to find the flying elephant, sleeping in a nest in the low-lying limbs of an enormous jujube tree. The maharaja raised the golden bow and took careful aim. The tip of the ruby arrow glittered in the first rays of morning sunlight. Haroom looked away.

"Suddenly, there came an intense, cacophonous alarm, as if every creature of Punjam Hy Loo knew of the maharaja's murderous intent. Charging down from the towers above came the Sisters of Flight, wings outstretched, with all manner of weapons at the ready—gleaming

swords, razor-sharp daggers, fantastical flying spears with wings of their own. It was a sight so beautiful, so terrifying that Haroom and the maharaja froze.

"Then the maharaja raised his bow again, this time aiming it at the Sisters of Flight. 'Look, Haroom, an even greater prize,' he exclaimed.

"In that single moment Haroom's whole life changed. He knew, for the very first time, what he wanted. He could not bear to see a Sister of Flight harmed. He ordered the maharaja to stop.

"The maharaja paid his servant no heed. He let loose the arrow. Haroom blocked it. Its ruby tip pierced his chest, and he crumbled to the ground.

"The maharaja stared in shock, then kneeled beside his fallen friend. Weeping, he tried to stop the flow of blood but could not. Haroom was dying.

The Sisters of Flight landed around them. The

most beautiful of the sisters, the one the maharaja had meant to kill, approached them. 'We did not know that any man could be so selfless,' she said. Her sisters nodded.

"With one hand, she grabbed the arrow and plucked it from Haroom's chest, then kissed her fingertips and gently touched his wound.

"Haroom stirred, and his eyes fluttered open. All he could see was the face of the Sister of Flight. And all she could see was the brave and noble Haroom.

"He was a slave no more.

"She took his hand, and in that instant her wings vanished.

"The other sisters lunged toward the maharaja in fury. They raised their swords, and Haroom could see they meant to kill his former master. 'He will no longer harm you,' he said. 'Please, let him go—send him on his way.'

"The sisters looked from one to the other, then agreed. But they declared that the maharaja must leave all he brought with him. The golden bow, the ruby-tipped arrow, the flying craft of teeth, and Haroom, his only friend.

"'And one thing more.

"'You must also leave your vanity and cruelty behind so that we can know and understand them.'

"The maharaja was heartbroken but agreed.

"The flying elephant glided down from his nest, and with his trunk, he touched the maharaja's fore-head, and all the vanity and cruelty went from him.

"But once these things were gone, there was little left—the maharaja was as simple as a baby monkey. In fact, he even sprouted a tail and scampered away speaking gibberish, shrinking to the size of an infant.

"His vanity and cruelty would never be forgotten—the flying elephant had them now, and an elephant never forgets. As for Haroom and the beautiful Sister of Flight, they were married and lived on in Punjam Hy Loo. Within a year, a child was born. A girl. Selfless like her father. Pure of heart like her mother. She was named Toothiana."

Toothiana as a child

CHAPTER TWELVE

The Story of Queen Toothiana Continues:
A Mystery of Wing and Madness

MR. QWERTY TOOK A sip of tea and continued:
"The child of Haroom and Rashmi (for that was
Toothiana's mother's name) seemed to be a normal
mortal child. As there were no other human children
living in Punjam Hy Loo, her parents thought it best
to raise her among other mortals, and so they settled
on the outskirts of a small village at the edge of the
jungle. The young girl was well loved and protected
and lived a simple, happy life until she was twelve and
lost her last baby tooth. That's when all her troubles
began."

"Troubles?" Katherine asked nervously.

"Yes, troubles," Mr. Qwerty said. "For when she lost her last baby tooth, Toothiana sprouted wings. By the end of this first miraculous day, she could fly with the speed of a bird, darting to the top of the tallest trees to choose the ripest mangoes, papayas, and starfruit for the children of the village. She played with the birds and made friends with the wind.

"But while the children delighted in Toothiana's new skill, the adults of the village were bewildered, even frightened, by this half bird, half girl. Some thought she was an evil spirit and should be killed; others saw ways to use her, as either a freak to be caged and paraded about, or to force her to fly to the palace of the new maharaja and steal his jewels.

"Haroom and Rashmi knew that to keep their daughter safe, they would have to pack their few belongings and escape. And so they did, deep into the jungle. The village children, all of whom adored Toothiana, tried to persuade their parents to leave her alone. But it was no use. The grown-ups of the village had gone mad with fear and greed.

"They built a large cage, hired the best hunters in the land, and asked them to capture the young girl. Among these was a hunter most mysterious. He spoke not a word and was shrouded from head to foot in tattered cloth stitched together with jungle vines. The villagers were wary of him, and even the other hunters found him peculiar. 'He knows the jungle better than any of us—it's as if he's more a creature than a man,' they remarked quietly among themselves.

"But Haroom and Rashmi were as wily as any hunter. Haroom, knowing everything there was to know about tracking, could disguise their trail so that no one could follow it. And Rashmi, who could converse with any animal, enlisted their aid in confounding the hunters. Tigers, elephants, even giant pythons would intercept the hunters whenever they neared. But the hunters, eager for the riches and fame they'd receive if they caged Toothi-ana, would not give up."

Why can grown-ups be so strange and wicked sometimes? Katherine wondered, not asking aloud so as not to stop Mr. Qwerty's story. He cleared his throat and continued.

"The children of the village were also determined to thwart the hunters. They defied their parents, sending word to Toothiana and her mother and father again and again whenever the hunters were stalking the jungle. Toothiana, wiser still, hid in the treetops by day, only visiting her parents in the darkest hours of the night.

"After weeks of the best hunters in the land failing to capture Toothiana, the cunning villagers became more sly. They secretly followed their children and discovered where Toothiana's parents were hiding. They left a trail of coins for the hunters to follow. But only one hunter came—the one they almost feared. It was then that the Mysterious Hunter finally spoke. His voice was strange, high-pitched, almost comical, but his words were cold as death. 'Seize the parents,' he snarled. 'Make it known that I will slit their throats if Toothiana does not surrender. That will bring this child of flight out of hiding.'

"His plan made sense; the villagers did as he suggested. They attacked Haroom and Rashmi's camp.

With so many against them, the two surrendered without a fight. They had told their clever daughter to never try and help them if they were ever captured.

"But the Mysterious Hunter had planned for that. He shouted out to any creature that could hear, 'The parents of the flying girl will die by dawn if she comes not!'

"The creatures of the jungle hurried to warn Toothiana that her parents were doomed if she did not come. Toothiana had never disobeyed her parents, but the thought of them at the dubious mercy of these grown-ups filled her with rage and determination, and she flew straight to her parents' aid. She dove down from the treetops, ready to kill any who would try to harm her parents.

"But Haroom and Rashmi were brave and cunning as well. Haroom, who had never harmed a living creature, was prepared to stop at nothing to prevent his daughter from being enslaved. And Rashmi, like all Sisters of Flight, had been a great warrior. As Toothiana neared, they slashed and fought like beings possessed. Toothiana flickered back and forth, hovering over her mother and father, reaching for them, but she did not have the strength to lift them up over the angry mob. Rashmi thrust a stringed pouch into her daughter's hands. 'Keep these to remember us by. Keep these to protect yourself,' she pleaded to her child.

"'Now go!' commanded her father. 'GO!'

"With a heartrending cry, the winged girl did as her father ordered. She flew away but stopped, unsure of what to do. Her ears filled with the sound of the vengeful mob falling upon her parents.

"'Go!' shouted her mother.

"Toothiana flew wildly and desperately away. And as she went, she screamed from the depths of her soul. It was the scream of two beings: human and animal. It was a scream so pained and fierce that it caused all the villagers who were attacking her parents to go briefly deaf. All except . . . the Mysterious Hunter. He screamed back to Toothiana. His was a scream equally unsettling—a scream of rage and hate that was more animal than human. Toothiana knew in that instant that she had a mortal enemy—one who she must kill or be killed by.

"But for now she would grieve. She flew to the highest treetop and huddled deep inside its foliage. She had no tears, only the blank ache of a now-empty life. She rocked back and forth in a trance of disbelief for a full day and night. Then she remembered the pouch her mother had thrust into her hands. Trembling, she opened it. Inside was a small box carved from a single giant ruby. It was covered in feathery patterns, and Toothiana knew that the box had once been the ruby-tipped arrow that had nearly killed her parents. Inside this beautiful box was a cluster of baby teeth and a note: —

Our Dearest Girl,

These are the teeth of your childhood. If you have them under your pillow as you sleep, or hold it tightly, you will remember that which you need — a memory of happy days, or of deepest hopes, or even of us in better times.

But one tooth is not yours. It is a tooth of amazing power, and from what being it comes from, we do not know.

Use it only in times of the greatest danger or need.

Your Dearest Parents

"Toothiana still did not cry, not even after reading the note. She slept with her baby teeth under her pillow and took solace in the dreams and memories it gave her."

CHAPTER THIRTEEN

Lost Teeth and a Purpose Found

Toothiana stayed in the jungle. She began to hate her wings. Once, she had thought them wondrous things, but now she saw them as the reason for the death of her parents. Her grief and loneliness knew no depths. The creatures of the jungle did what they could to help her, by bringing her food and making her treetop sleeping places as comfortable as possible. The children of the village tried to aid as well, but they now had to be doubly cautious of the village grown-ups.

"As for Toothiana, she became more and more

convinced that she belonged nowhere—not among the creatures of the jungle and certainly not among the humans of the village. She was alone. When she was at her very saddest, she would take one of her baby teeth from the carved box she always carried in her mother's pouch she now wore around her neck, and hold it until it revealed its memories.

"As the lonely years passed, Toothiana saw that the village children lost much of their innocence and some of their goodness as they grew up. She began to collect their teeth, so that, in the future, she could give them back their childhood memories and remind them of their kindness, just as her own parents had done for her.

"Soon the children, not wanting their parents to find out, began to hide their lost teeth under their pil-lows for Toothiana to find. And she, cheered by this new game of sorts, began in turn to leave behind small bits of treasure she had found in the jungle. A gold nugget here. A sprinkling of sapphire chips there.

"But you can imagine the curiosity that is stirred when a five-year-old sits down to breakfast with an uncut ruby in her palm, or when a ten-year-old boy comes to the table with a pocket full of emeralds. Once again the hearts of the grown-ups filled with greed, and it wasn't long before they forced their children to tell them how they had come upon those treasures. Soon enough they had laid a new trap for Toothiana.

"One dark, cloudy night Toothiana flew to the village to make her nightly rounds. A boy named Akela had lost his two front teeth, and Toothiana had a special treasure saved for him: two beautiful uncut diamonds. But as she entered his open window, it wasn't Akela she found. Instead the Mysterious Hunter leaped toward her. From behind his shroud of rags, she could see the strangest eyes. Close together. Beady. Not entirely human. And cold with hate.

"Toothiana's rage clouded her keen intellect. All she could think was, *I must get rid of this . . . thing!* But before she could act, a steel door slammed down between her and the Hunter. She glanced around with birdlike quickness. The room was not Akela's bedroom, but, in fact, a cleverly disguised steel cage.

"She was trapped! The villagers cheered as the Hunter hauled away the cage. His platoon of slave-like helpers pulled the wheeled prison away from the villagers and into the jungle. The helpers were as strangely shrouded as the Hunter who commanded them was, and seemed excited by the capture. The children wept, begging their parents to let Toothiana go free. But they would not. The Mysterious Hunter had promised them riches beyond their dreams when he sold Toothiana.

"Toothiana flung herself wildly against the cage, like a cornered eagle. But it did no good. The Hunter and his minions traveled swiftly through the night, deeper into the jungle. They knew the creatures of the wild would try to help Toothiana, so they carried the one weapon every animal fears: fire.

"Torches were lashed to the roof of Toothiana's cage. The Mysterious Hunter himself carried the brightest torch of all. The animals kept their distance, but they continued to follow the eerie caravan and keep watch over Toothiana, waiting for a chance to strike.

"After days of travel they arrived at the base of the steep mountain of Toothiana's birthplace—the kingdom of Punjam Hy Loo. The great elephants that guarded the mountain were standing at the ready, shifting back and forth on their massive feet. Toothiana's jungle friends had warned them that the Mysterious Hunter was headed their way.

"The Hunter did not challenge the elephants. He ordered his minions to halt and made no move to attack. Instead, he held his flaming torch aloft. 'I bring a treasure to the Sisters of Flight and the flying elephant king who dwell in Punjam Hy Loo!' he shouted into the night sky. The sky was empty; there was no sign of either the winged women who ruled there, or of the flying elephant.

"The Hunter called out again. 'I bring you the half-breed daughter of Haroom and Rashmi.' At this, an otherworldly sound—like a rustle of trees in the wind—was heard. And indeed wind did begin to blow down from the mountain. It grew stronger and more furious, with gusts that nearly put out the torches.

"Toothiana knew instinctually that this wind was sent by the Sisters of Flight and that they did not trust the Hunter. She also knew that it was time to take out the box her parents had left her.

"As the winds continued to rise, the Hunter grew increasingly nervous, as did his minions. They began to chatter in the oddest way, not in words, but in sounds.

"Then a chorus of voices, all speaking in unison, rang out bright and clear above the howl of the wind: 'Tell us, Hunter, why cage our child? Where be her father and mother? What trick of men do you bring us? What do you seek, you who seem of men and yet are not?'

"The Hunter rocked on his feet, seething with undisguised hate. He held his torch high and stepped forward, leaning into the wind. The elephants raised their trunks but took a step back. Fire was a fearsome thing, even for these mighty beasts.

"The Hunter laughed, then threw down his tattered cloak. He was no man at all, but a massive monkey. 'A maharaja of men I once was,' he screamed, 'and by your doing, I am now a king of the monkeys!' Then his troops dropped their cloaks as well. An array of monkeys revealed themselves, all armed with bows and arrows.

"The Monkey King shrieked above the roaring wind, 'You ask about her parents? Dead! By *my* doing! What do I seek? Revenge! On all who made me thus!' Then he threw his torch into the herd of elephants and grabbed a bow and arrow from one of his men. He had it drawn in an instant, aimed directly at Toothiana's heart.

"Before he could let loose the arrow, the wind tripled in strength. Toothiana knew what to do. She held the ruby box tightly in her hand. 'Mother, Father, help me,' she whispered furiously, clenching her eyes shut. She pictured them clearly in her mind, letting herself feel the bond they had shared so deeply, letting herself remember how much they had sacrificed for her.

"Suddenly, she was no longer in the cage. She was no longer a single entity, but several smaller versions of herself.

"Bow drawn, the Monkey King hesitated, bewildered. *How can this be?* He could not remember the power of love—even though it had been this girl's father who had loved him best—and his own memories were now fueled only by hate.

"So the world turned against him once again.

"The Sisters of Flight circled overhead. It was the flapping of their wings that made the great wind. It grew wilder and stranger, like a tornado. Leaves snapped off trees. Dirt swirled like a storm, and the Monkey King's torch blew out.

"Now the only light came from the Moon, and no jungle creature fears that guiding light. In an instant the elephants stampeded forward. Toothiana's animal friends attacked. Toothiana's mini-selves charged the Monkey King. The monkey army screamed and ran.

"The king tried to grab the Toothianas, but he could not catch them. Then all the fairy-sized selves merged back into a single being.

A mini Tooth

Toothiana was mystified by her new power, but she didn't think on it. With one hand, she grabbed the Monkey King by the throat. It was as if she now had the strength of a dozen. The Monkey King cried out in terror and pain.

"For an instant Toothiana felt the rage within her swell. She would snap his neck and be done with him. But the little box glowed in one hand, and the memory of her parents made her stop. She would not end this monkey man's life. Let the jungle choose his fate.

"So she let him go.

"He fell to the ground, and she did not look back as she flew up to join the Sisters of Flight.

"As they sped away, Toothiana and her kindred could hear the creatures of the jungle do as they saw fit with the fallen Monkey King. And his cries could be heard all the way to the Moon."

Mr. Qwerty then shut his pages. The tale, as it was written, was done.

Toothiana's story made Katherine feel many things, but the strangest was a twinge of envy. *Toothiana* had memories of *her* parents. It was something Katherine wished for more than anything.

CHAPTER FOURTEEN

Nightlight Faces the Unknown

AFTER LISTENING AT THE window to the story of Queen Toothiana, Nightlight flew listlessly around the mountains that surrounded the Lunar Lamadary. He was increasingly troubled. Until now he had viewed the events of his life in very simple terms. To him, the world was divided into good and bad. Katherine and the Guardians were good—absolutely. And Pitch was bad, through and through, without even an ounce of good in him. And yet . . .

Nightlight was confounded by what he had seen in Katherine's Dream Tear. And in this dream, Pitch's hand was human, as it had been since he'd tried to make Nightlight a Darkling Prince.

But there was more.

In the dream, Pitch had held in his human hand the locket with his daughter's picture. But the picture shifted, and Katherine's face took its place. And then *her* face began to change! It became different. Older. A grown-up's face. And then darker. More like Pitch's.

Nightlight was afraid of this dream. It felt true. No Guardian had seen any sign of Pitch of late, yet Nightlight had; Pitch *lived*—in Katherine's dreams. What did this mean?

Would she grow up? Would she become like so many adults, a grim shadow of her youthful self? Or was there a greater danger? Would she somehow be taken over by Pitch? Was her soul in danger? These questions tore at his heart and soul in ways he could not comprehend or put into words. So he turned to his oldest friend.

For hours he waited for the Moon to rise, and when it did, he took Katherine's Dream Tear and held it up. The moonbeam inside his staff began to flash, and moments later, the Man in the Moon responded to his signal. Moonbeams shined down and flickered as they interpreted the Dream Tear. Then Nightlight, waiting anxiously, finally whispered in his rarely used and otherworldly voice, "Will my Katherine go Darkling or stay true?" He stood, still and tense, for a long while until a moonbeam brought back the simple answer, the answer that was the truth of everything:

Believe. Believe. Believe, it said.

And for the first time in his endless childhood life, Nightlight cried. He was not sure why he was crying.

He could not describe the feeling that brought the tears. It was not happiness or sorrow. It was not good or bad. But it was something just as powerful.

Someday he would know what it was, that first mysterious step beyond childhood. It is a strange feeling, to realize that you will grow up, especially for one who has been a child for so long. But he now had the answer he needed to face this uncertainty.

Believe. Believe. Believe. If he could remember that, he would make everything right. And so his tears stopped. He wiped them from his cheeks, then brought them close to his face, so unaccustomed was he to having tears.

Each was bright with light and seemed to take the burden from his anxious heart. He let them spill together with Katherine's Dream Tear.

Then he took the diamond tip of his staff and

touched it to the tears, holding it there until they fused with the diamond. Now the spearlike point of his staff held not just his friend's fear and sorrow, but his own as well.

The moonbeam inside grew furiously bright, for sorrow and fear that are triumphed over make a powerful weapon.

At that instant he heard Katherine calling for him, and he knew that whatever might come, he was ready.

CHAPTER FIFTEEN

Plots, Plans, and Pillows

IT IS NOT EASY to fall asleep when an entire village, an army of Abominable Snowmen, a troupe of ancient Lunar holy men, and all your best friends are coming into your bedroom and wishing you good night. It is also not easy to sleep when you know you are going to be visited by a half-bird, half-human queen with magical powers. And it is really hard to sleep when you have made a secret plan with your dearest friend to do the *one thing* you've been told you absolutely MUST NOT DO when this particular queen arrives. So there Katherine sat, in her huge and feathered bed in her special room in the Lunar Lamadary, as wide awake as any twelve-year-old has ever been.

She'd just checked under her pillow for the eleventh time to make certain that her tooth hadn't somehow rolled onto the floor when North opened the bedroom door again, just enough to stick in his head. "Still awake?" he asked in surprise.

Ombric and Bunnymund crowded in next to him, crammed so tightly in the doorway that Katherine could see only half of Ombric's face and one of Bunnymund's ears, with Ombric's beard tangled around it.

"Perhaps if you chant the ancient Atlantan phrase 'Sleep-o deep-o slumberly doo—'" Ombric began to suggest.

Bunnymund interrupted with, "Counting! That'll do it. Count chocolate eggs jumping counterclockwise over a small wall also made of chocolate—"

Then North interrupted, saying, "A song! We should sing a song!"

Then they all began to talk at once: "It should be about eggs! A sleepy chocolate egg opera would be perfect!" . . . "No, no, no! A good old-fashioned Cossack lullaby. 'Don't cut my throat while I am sleeping, mother, my mother dear.'" . . . "North, that's awful! No, she should chant, 'Dream, dream, dream of chocolate ocean waves . . .'"

And so it went till Nightlight flew down from the rafters and, with a firm but caring swing of his staff, slammed the door shut.

The three Guardians muttered outside the door for a moment or two, then the Lunar Lamas could be heard suggesting that the centuries-old method of simply being left quietly alone tended to bring about sleep quite reliably. And so things finally settled down.

Nightlight leaped to Katherine's bed and sat cross-legged on the footboard. He still seemed . . . different to her; no longer quite so sad or distant. But the cheerful half grin that had always been there was replaced by a look that seemed—well, she couldn't really put a finger on it, but he didn't seem quite so like a little boy now.

And whether it was the Lamas' suggestion or just the result of a very full day, Katherine suddenly felt overcome with sleepiness and ready to close her eyes. But she propped herself up on one elbow for another minute, careful not to shift the pillow that covered her tooth. She wanted to go over the plan she'd concocted earlier with Nightlight one more time. It had come to her when the Lunar Lamas had told her even more details about the workings of Queen Toothiana. It had taken a while, given the Lamas' propensity for vague answers, but Katherine had learned that she had to be asleep for Toothiana to come and take her tooth. And only Toothiana could unlock the countless memories in a tooth, by holding it in her magic grasp. Once the memories were unlocked, Katherine wanted her tooth back.

"You must get my tooth back the instant she does her magic!" she reminded Nightlight.

Nightlight nodded. He could feel how much this meant to Katherine. *She wants to remember her mother and father,* thought Nightlight. *And if she remembers them, then perhaps she'll forget Pitch.*

That's what he believed in his hopeful heart. He had never failed Katherine before, and he would not fail her now.

CHAPTER SIXTEEN

In Which We See the Extremely Secret Process by Which a Tooth Is Gathered

FOR CENTURY UPON CENTURY Queen Toothiana flew majestically on her nightly rounds with her half dozen mini-selves. At the bedside of every child who had left a tooth under his pillow, one of her selves quietly collected the tooth and made a silent wish. The children each were different, but the wish was the same: that the child would grow up to be kind and happy. In the many villages and cities and jungles of Asia, the children knew to place their lost teeth under their pillows. Then a tiny treasure would be left in place of the tooth. And the tooth would be stored in the palace of the flying elephant of Punjam Hy Loo until it was needed again.

Once, Toothiana had loved to spend time at each child's bedside—straightening a blanket that had been kicked off or whispering messages of hope into sleeping ears. She had loved to peek from the windows as the children woke in the morning; their joyful cries when they reached under their pillows and found their gifts—this was *her* treasure.

But she wanted to help all the children in the world, however there simply wasn't enough of her to go around. Since she'd learned long ago that jewels of any kind were likely to bring the wrong kind of interest from adults, she had begun to use coins or other smaller treasures in exchange for teeth. But, oh, the coins! Children loved to receive them; however, as more countries were formed, more currencies were invented, and each child required the coin from his or her realm. It became a complicated business. Even with six of her, there was barely time to outrun the coming dawn.

Yet despite Queen Toothiana's hurried pace, there was something about her presence that calmed every child she visited. And while on any given night she might encounter a bad dream or two, the terrible time of the Nightmare Man seemed to be over. The children in her lands, like children everywhere, called him the Boogeyman, and she'd seen no sign of him for months.

While Queen Toothiana knew less about the Guardians than they knew about her, she'd observed that glimmering boy made of light who had been involved in battling the Boogeyman. She'd seen how brave he'd been saving the girl who wrote stories and drew pictures. She felt a special fondness for the two of them. In a strange way their devotion to each other reminded her of her parents' devotion, and so she was looking very much forward to the last stop of the evening.

For the very first time, she'd received a call to the highest peak in the Himalayas—to the Lunar Lamadary. There, she knew she would find out more about this valiant girl who rode on a giant goose.

Meanwhile, Nightlight waited for Queen Toothiana on the top of the Lamadary's tower with as much patience as he could muster. He remembered the first time he had seen the bird woman: He'd been playing moonbeam tag when she'd flickered by so quickly that he mistook her for an enormous hummingbird. And from time to time they glimpsed each other. She'd never spoken to him, but she always nodded whenever their flying paths briefly crossed. But Nightlight, with his keen intuition, sensed that she distrusted most people and didn't want the other Guardians to know about her, so he had kept his knowledge of her to himself. Besides, there was something about her that made him feel sort of shy.

But Katherine asked for his help. So he kept his eyes trained on the night sky, peering among the bright stars for the first sign of this Toothiana.

Soon, Nightlight spied a glow. It was a shimmer—flickering sparks of iridescent blues and greens. As it came closer, Nightlight made out a feathered head, bright green eyes, and a happy smile. He tried to hide, but Toothiana and her mini-selves saw him before he could leap into the shadows.

Toothiana knew immediately that he was up to

something. Through the centuries, too many children had plotted and planned to wake at the moment she arrived for her to be caught unawares now. She shook her head sternly and held a finger to her lips, warning him not to interfere.

Nightlight wavered. His deepest loyalty rested with Katherine, and yet he found himself acutely aware that he needed to trust this winged being. At least for the moment. With the slightest of nods, he let her know that he would do as she asked. But he followed her closely as she and her selves shot through the window and down to Katherine's bed.

Three of the mini-selves, no bigger than sparrows, each carried a gold coin. They flew silently to Katherine's pillow, then tucked in their wings and crawled gently and silently under it. Another landed by Katherine's ear and plucked at a tiny silver instrument

Katherine and her visitors

while she sang a soft, lulling song. Nightlight was fascinated. *They sing to make her sleep more soundly*, he realized.

Another mini-self stood guard by the pillow while the last one winged about the room and seemed to be keeping watch as Toothiana, an expectant smile upon her face, waited for the tooth to be smuggled from under the pillow.

The pillow puckered here and rumpled there, then, at last, the three small fairies emerged, Katherine's tooth in hand. Toothiana picked it up tenderly. With her other hand, she brought out a beautiful, carved, ruby box from a pouch she wore around her neck, and held it tightly.

She closed her eyes as if in deep thought. A glow began to emanate from both Katherine's tooth and the box. The queen's magical power seemed to be working.

Nightlight had seen all he needed. As willful as the flying woman seemed, he would do as Katherine asked. He readied himself to swoop in to take the tooth, but a quiet, mournful sigh from Toothiana made him pause, puzzled. A sadness came over her lovely face, and then her mini-selves sighed as well, as though they shared her every feelings. She could see all of Katherine's memories.

Toothiana murmured, "Poor child. You're like me—you've lost your mother and father. But . . . you didn't even have a chance to know or remember them." She bowed her head ever so slightly and looked down at Katherine, who slept on.

"I must give you the memory you long for," she whispered. Nightlight leaned forward anxiously as Toothiana lowered the hand that held the tooth to Katherine's forehead.

Nightlight knew he needn't steal the tooth now. Katherine would have the memory. He was glad. He felt a peculiar bond with this bird royal and didn't want to anger her.

But suddenly, a sound most angry stopped Toothiana from granting Katherine her wish.

CHAPTER SEVENTEEN

Monkey See, Monkey Don't

MONKEYS, DOZENS OF THEM, sprang through the windows of Katherine's room and swarmed the chamber. They were huge, hulking, and armed with daggers, spears, and crude weapons.

What is this dark business? Toothiana wondered in shock as a handful of the malicious creatures, screeching loudly, leaped upon her with a swiftness that was unnatural. She crammed the ruby box back into its pouch, then turned, batting her wings at the fiends as she tried to escape their grip, then drew her swords and slashed away. But the monkeys were too quick.

Katherine startled awake and instinctively grabbed for the dagger on her night table as six or eight of her attackers grasped her arms and legs. A monkey with a grotesquely humanlike face pressed his hand against her mouth so that she could not cry out. Nightlight was there in a flash, batting the animals away with his staff, but for each monkey he hit, seven would take its place. The room was overrun with chattering, maniacal monster monkeys.

Queen Toothiana knew she had to protect the girl. As Katherine struggled to free herself, Toothiana lunged for the monkeys. In the tangle of tails and clawing hands, Katherine's tooth was knocked to the floor. Both Toothiana and Katherine cried out at the same time.

Katherine was determined not to lose that tooth. She elbowed one monkey after another, reaching,

reaching, reaching for the tooth. Each time her fingers nearly gripped it, it was kicked away. Katherine darted along the floor on her hands and knees, her eyes never leaving the tooth. Finally, it was within her grasp. One great last stretch, then—got it!

Only then, when her precious tooth was safely tucked in her palm, did Katherine think to scream, to call out for help. She didn't get a chance. Once again a hand covered her mouth. Then another had her leg; another, her arm.

Katherine strained against her captors, trying to squirm away as Toothiana and Nightlight struck at monkey after monkey. The tiny versions of Toothiana dove and charged relentlessly at the primates' eyes. They were making headway when a second wave of monkeys attacked. There were just too many.

The largest monkey, the one who seemed the

leader, snatched the pouch from around Toothiana's neck, raised it over his head, and hurled it to one of his minions, who promptly leaped out the window with the prize, followed by a dark mass of his scuffling cohorts.

Toothiana struggled to follow them, sweeping her wings at the monkeys in her way, but then she stopped short. The monkey who had taken her precious box—she recognized him! *That vile creature . . . That monkey was the one who . . .* Toothiana's rage took hold, and in one swift move, she had him in her grip.

The room became a cyclone of monkeys; they stampeded around the walls and began to bound out the windows in waves. They seemed to be running right across the night sky, as if it had become solid under their feet. And then in a flash of darkness, the monkeys vanished.

All except one.

Toothiana pressed her sword against her old enemy's throat, breathing hard.

The door flew open. North burst into the room, with Ombric, Bunnymund, Yaloo and his Yeti lieutenants, and even a few sleepy-eyed Lamas right behind him.

"Villains, explain yourselves!" North demanded, his cutlass ready.

Toothiana didn't respond. Nor did she remove her blade from the monkey's neck.

North took a step closer, and Toothiana cocked her head, birdlike, from right to left. As North took another step, her feathers flared up, as if to warn him not to come closer. One of her wings hung limp.

The captive monkey, frantic-eyed, whimpered something that sounded vaguely like "Help!"

Everyone froze, wonderstruck at the sight of the flying woman they had heard so much about. They had expected a serene being, but here she was in fighting stance and with a death grip on a decidedly evil-looking ape. Ombric was madly sorting through the various dialects of primate languages to best question the captive monkey. *Odd how humanlike it looks*, he thought. *Very odd indeed.*

In all the confusion, it was Nightlight who was the first to notice that Katherine was not in her bed.

Before he could alert the others, they all felt the surge of his frantic worry.

North whipped his head back and forth, surveying the room. "Katherine?" he called. Then "KATHERINE!" Dread crept through the Guardians when there came no reply.

Ombric and Bunnymund reached out to her with

their minds, but they got only a confusing darkness in response.

North turned his attention back to Toothiana and the strange creatures she held prisoner. He glared menacingly at them, raising his sword.

"Tell me what you've done with Katherine," he demanded, "or you will never take another breath."

CHAPTER EIGHTEEN

A Journey Most Confounding, with Flying Monkeys Who Smell Very Badly Indeed

KATHERINE CLUTCHED HER TOOTH as she tried to push away the putrid cloak that one of the monkeys had thrown over her head. The last thing she had seen had been the monkey with the humanlike face take Toothiana's pouch. Then it dawned on her. *That must be the Monkey King from Toothiana's story!*

The air felt colder, so Katherine knew she had been dragged outside. Her mind raced with so many questions, she hardly had time to be scared. *The Monkey King has come for revenge, but why take me?* she wondered. She felt herself being prodded and shoved and sometimes even thrown from one tight grip to another, speeding along at an impossibly fast pace. The monkeys seemed to be running on solid ground, but sometimes it felt like they were—what? Flying? She pulled at the cloak till she made a small hole. Clouds. Stars. Sky. They *were* flying! And were extremely high.

At that moment the cloak slipped to one side, and Katherine caught a glimpse of solid surface below— a road made of shadows. She gasped. It was like Nightlight's roads of light, but inky and frightening. *There's only one being who could make a sky road of shadows,* she realized with dread.

And then she remembered her dream, her awful dream.

Screeching incessantly, the monkeys sped on. Katherine tried to reach out to her friends with her mind, but something about this dark highway was blocking her thoughts.

Her breath formed tiny icicles around her face and nose as freezing air rushed past. She ripped the hole bigger and was finally able to take a deep, unfettered breath, but it was too cold, and she pulled the cloak shut, now feeling smothered again.

The monkeys had a stink to them that she hadn't expected; they'd looked much sweeter in the pictures from Ombric's ancient book. A fleeting wish that she had taken the time to learn the language of monkeys flashed through her mind. Ombric could speak it, no doubt, but as there were no monkeys in Santoff Claussen, it had seemed much more important to learn languages she could actually use—like squirrel and Lunar Moth. She could likely learn it easily enough. She'd learned Great Snow Goose, hadn't she?

Oh, Kailash! Katherine thought with a groan. *She will be so worried. Nightlight, too.* Then it struck her: What if he were wounded? A wave of fear for her friends swept over her, forcing her attention back to the dilemma at hand. She kicked and pushed against the cloak, but it was futile. The monkeys simply held it tighter around her, until she could barely move her arms.

The temperature was changing again, slowly at first and then more quickly. The icy air warmed. The cloak felt suffocating. Katherine's stomach lurched as the monkeys took a giant leap and then bounced up and down on what felt like a tree branch.

The cloak slipped from her head. This time the monkeys made no effort to cover her face as they swung from tree to tree, dragging Katherine along with them. Sometimes it seemed the branches could never hold them, and then they'd plummet down, down, down, in rapid falls, leaves slapping at Katherine's face and neck. She found herself being thrown from one paw to the next until one of the monkeys would grab a solid branch and begin the ascent again.

Besides the screeching monkeys—were they *ever* quiet?—Katherine saw no other jungle creatures at all, not even birds. It was as if the monkeys were the only animals in this land. *Where are the other animals?* she wondered. *Where are the elephants and the tigers? The snakes and the lizards?*

And then, without warning, the monkeys let go of their grasp and dropped Katherine. She didn't fall far. Just a few feet. When she realized she was unhurt, she began to cautiously look around. She could not see much beneath the jungle canopy, but she was able to pick out what seemed to be the ruins of what once must have been a magnificent city. The jungle had done its best to take it over, but Katherine could see evidence of the city's former glory in the tarnished gold and silver fixtures on the crumbling walls.

Where in the world am I? She looked in every direction and didn't see a soul, just the army of monkeys. But now they kept their distance. It had become eerily quiet. So Katherine decided there was nothing to do but investigate. She headed for the closest buildings, stopping at the first to peer at a dirt-covered mosaic. The design, though half buried under a layer of mud and mold, looked exquisite, so using the side of her fist, she wiped the muck off until she could make out the outline of an elephant—an elephant with wings.

"The flying elephant!" she said with a gasp. *I'm in Punjam Hy Loo!* It seemed almost a dream. Just yesterday Mr. Qwerty had told them all about this city and the Sisters of Flight!

She looked in every direction. *Were the sisters still here somewhere? What has brought this city so low? Were there still elephants guarding the mountain?* She looked for more clues and didn't notice that the shadows around her were growing larger. Blacker. She didn't see that hundreds more monkeys were quietly perching on the derelict walls surrounding her.

It wasn't until an immense shadow loomed directly over her that Katherine looked up and gulped. It was as she feared.

"Pitch," she said, trying to sound calm.

The Nightmare King greeted her with a ghoulish smile. "Greetings, my Darkling Daughter," he whispered in a voice that was anything but welcoming.

CHAPTER NINETEEN

Panic in the Himalayas

"WHERE IS KATHERINE?" NORTH roared again at the winged woman in front of him. He was sure she had some hand in Katherine's disappearance, but his sword was pulling away from this strange being—he'd almost forgotten how the sword, the first relic from the Man in the Moon, could tell friend from foe. The sword knew Toothiana meant no harm to any Guardian. But North resisted it. The woman knew something, and she must tell them.

Nightlight sat on Katherine's bed. Her pillow had been tossed to the floor, but the three coins that had been left for her were still in place.

Toothiana's eyes darted from North to the others, one hand still tight around the struggling monkey's neck, the other still clasping her sword, poised and ready to end this creature's life. With a quick glance, she told her mini-selves to stay back. Her feathers fluffed and quivered. *With rage?* North wondered. *Or panic?*

He had seen that look before. As a boy in the wild, he had known it well. It was the look of a trapped animal, one that had nothing to lose, so would go down fighting. North had learned how to approach them—calmly and carefully.

Then it dawned on North how he and the others must appear to her—this queen who had every reason to mistrust adults. She was facing a sword-wielding warrior, a seven-foot-tall bunny, an ancient

wizard, and Abominable Snowmen bearing all manner of weapons. The set of Toothiana's jaw was fierce,
but her eyes, almond-shaped and green, betrayed her.
Why, she must feel just like a sparrow caught in a cage,
he thought.

So North held up one hand and sheathed his
sword. He approached the queen slowly. Even the
monkey stopped his squirming as North took one
careful step after another, never blinking, never taking his eyes off her.

"We mean you no harm," North said in his most
soothing voice. "But we are most anxious to find our
friend—the girl you were here to see tonight. Do you
know what happened to her?"

Toothiana cocked her head, held North's gaze in
her own for the longest time, then seemed to make a
decision: She would trust this hulking man.

"Gone. Taken," she said.

"Taken where? By whom?" North encouraged, forcing his voice to stay steady.

"*This* creature knows," she said, gesturing toward the monkey.

Ombric made one cautious step forward. "Is that creature the Monkey King?" he asked, recalling Toothiana's story.

She nodded, then gave the creature a hard shake. "Tell what you know!"

The monkey spat at her. "Never!" he screeched.

North could scarcely contain himself. "Tell us!" he roared. "Or die!"

The monkey merely sucked on his teeth and smirked.

Toothiana grabbed the simian by his feet and swung him upside down, giving him a good shake with each word. "Where. Is. The. Girl? Where. Is. My. Box?"

"Gone. Taken," the Monkey King mimicked.

North unsheathed his sword and brought its tip to the monkey's chin.

The Monkey King simply continued to suck on his teeth, as if being held upside down with a sword pressed to his chin was a perfectly normal course of events.

Bunnymund's whiskers bristled. He, too, knew the ways of animals, even better than North did. And North—like all poor humans—was beginning to let his emotions get the best of him. It was time for cooler heads. It was time for the Pooka to take charge.

He pressed a paw on North's arm until North lowered his sword. Then he eyed the monkey appraisingly. "You're very clever," the Pooka told him. "Clever enough to fool all of us. To break into the Lamadary. To lead your troops to capture our friend. And steal this lady's precious treasure."

While he was talking, he was pulling a chocolate egg out of his pocket and carefully peeling it, as one would a piece of fruit. The aroma of a perfectly ripe banana, tinged with the scent of milky chocolate, filled the room.

Bunnymund motioned to Toothiana to turn the monkey right side up again. As she did, the monkey's eyes began to gleam. He reached for the chocolate, which Bunnymund dropped into his hand. Popping the confection into his mouth, the Monkey King closed his eyes. "Yum-yum," he said blissfully.

Nightlight watched closely. He had never before wanted to harm a creature of flesh and blood. Pitch was darkness, a phantom, but the monkey man was *alive*—a living being. Nightlight saw the hate in Toothiana's eyes for this creature. And in North's. Even Ombric's. And now he felt it too. And he did not like it.

The Monkey King motioned for another chocolate as Nightlight fought the urge to spear him through with his staff.

"What a wise monkey king. You want more. And more you'll have," Bunnymund said, patting his pockets and backing away. "But first you must answer our questions."

The Monkey King bobbed his head up and down

and answered in the language of monkeys.

Ombric translated. "The King of the Monkeys claims he is much too clever to fall for our tricks."

The monkey's eyes widened. He had never before met a human who could speak monkey.

"You are indeed clever, Maharaja," Ombric said, "but perhaps not as clever as you think you are. Who sent you to kidnap our friend?"

"No one sent me," the monkey said, speaking in the language of men. He raised his head haughtily. "I am a king. I lead my army where I choose. I am not 'sent.' And now I demand to be fed."

"Some army," North scoffed. "They've left you behind."

"They have not!" he howled.

"Then where oh where have they gone?" asked Bunnymund.

No longer a maharajah,
the Monkey King is maha-rose.

The Monkey King stiffened. "They'll be back."

Bunnymund took out another chocolate with a flourish and held it close to the Monkey King's nose.

"You'll get no more answers from me, *Rabbit Man,*" the Monkey King spat.

"Then no more yummies for you," said Bunnymund. He handed the chocolate to Ombric, who peeled tantalizingly, then bit it in half. The banana-laced fragrance filled the room.

The monkey eyed the other half of the chocolate and whimpered, "More yum-yum." Bunnymund shook his head.

"I *can't* tell you," the Monkey King whimpered. "I will be killed until dead."

"Who would dare do such a thing to such a clever Monkey King?" Ombric asked, searching for an even tone, though alarm bells were exploding in his head.

The Monkey King saw a chance to bargain. He drew himself up again. "One who can make me human again—make me much, much maharaja. Can *you* do that?"

North was growing tired of this back-and-forth. The longer this went on, the farther away Katherine could be taken. He leaped forward and smashed the monkey onto the floor. "Tell us what we ask!" he demanded.

The monkey giggled and pointed at Toothiana. "In *her* home. They wait at Punjam Hy Loo."

Toothiana trembled with rage. "You lie!"

"No, no, no," cackled the monkey. " 'Tis all part of the plan!"

"Coward!" North spat out, pacing in front of him. "You're a pathetic excuse for a king."

"And always have been," Toothiana added.

The Monkey King scowled darkly, his anger building. "Wait until the King of Nightmares makes me the King of Mans again. I will kill you deader than your father!"

Toothiana pulled her sword to his head. How dare he boast of such things in her presence!

But North and the other Guardians barely noticed. The words "King of Nightmares" had stilled them. North ceased pacing; Nightlight glowed brightly. Bunnymund's whiskers twitched, and Ombric's beard began to curl with worry. They all had only one thought.

Pitch was back!

"What does the Nightmare King want with my ruby box?" Toothiana asked now.

"And why take Katherine and leave the rest of us?" North demanded.

The Monkey King's eyes gleamed with triumph. "He seeks to build an army. And turn the girl into his Darkling Princess."

CHAPTER TWENTY

In Which Toothiana Makes a Startling Discovery

INSTANTLY THE GUARDIANS BEGAN to talk in low, tense voices. Queen Toothiana, however, kept her eyes trained on the Monkey King.

The Monkey King looked back at her with a gloat of self-importance.

Toothiana's eyes narrowed; her anger felt venomous. She thought about all of her years on the run. About her parents' deaths. Every sorrow of her life had been caused by this pathetic monkey.

He tried to avert her gaze, but Toothiana grabbed him by the neck again and forced him to look at her.

"How?" she demanded. "How did the jungle law spare you?"

The Monkey King glared at her, his eyes matching her own in the fury they contained. "The tigers tore at me. The serpents bit me. Every creature gave me wounds, but I would not die, for I had to destroy . . . YOU!"

"My father *saved* you," said Toothiana.

The Monkey King glanced away, drawing in a shaky breath.

Toothiana wondered if there was anything about this monkey worth sparing. Her father had saved him once, and he had been repaid with angry mobs and an early death. Did this monkey maharaja have even a shred of his childlike goodness left? There was only one way to know for sure. With an angry cry, Toothiana pried open the Monkey King's mouth.

"No baby teeth!" she shouted. "You die."

The monkey yowled, wrenching his jaw from her hands.

Toothiana swung her sword to strike a deadly blow when North bounded across the room and grabbed her wrist.

"No!" he yelled. "We need the creature. He can help us rescue our friend."

She scoffed at him. This monkey would never help anyone but himself. She lowered her sword.

"I'll leave," she said. "For Punjam Hy Loo. I'll get the ruby box *and* your girl."

"Pitch—he's crueler and more devious than you'd ever imagine," North warned. "You can't go alone."

"We'll come with you," Ombric implored. "Together our power is mighty."

Toothiana scoffed again. "This Pitch scares me not

at all." With that, she leaped onto the windowsill and prepared to spring into the air. But as she spread her wings, she listed to the left. Her right wing, her beautiful, iridescent right wing, hung limp.

CHAPTER TWENTY-ONE

Nightlight Sees a Woman of Mystery

KATHERINE TRAPPED AND ALONE with the Nightmare King was the worst thing Nightlight could possibly imagine.

For a new fear gripped him, one that he could not describe even to himself, for it was a feeling beyond his own understanding. But he knew that Katherine longed for a father's love and that Pitch had lost a daughter. Could this be a dangerous thing for his friend? He thought of what he'd seen in the Dream Tear and shook his head.

As he sat at the tower top, he looked up to the

Moon for reassurance, but it was blocked by dense, fast-moving clouds. There was a strange wind blowing, and Nightlight couldn't shake the feeling that he was being watched; even that his thoughts were somehow overheard. He'd had this feeling before. It was only when he was alone, and it did not seem threatening—but it was strange. He sometimes thought he saw a face—a woman's face, for just an instant—in the shapes of the clouds or in a swirl of leaves that blew past him or even in a mist of falling snowflakes. He never saw it clearly, and he wondered if it was just his daydreaming ways that made him think he even glimpsed this woman, but this time he looked about, trying to see if she was really there. He knew he felt something. He knew it felt tied somehow to Katherine and Pitch. He let his thoughts reach out, as they could with Katherine, but there was no response.

Just a vague feeling that someone, not unfriendly, was watching and waiting.

Nightlight paced about nervously. He needed to calm down, he needed a moment of peace, for his mind was not ready for all these strange feelings and grown-up thoughts. He didn't know what to do. How could he help Katherine? Should he fly pell-mell into the unknown and try to save her on his own? He was brave and clever enough—but this time he felt that it would take more than he could manage. He thought of the Bird Lady, Toothiana, this queen with a mother's heart and a warrior's ways—maybe she would know the trick of saving Katherine. But her wing was hurting and she could not fly.

Then he thought of Kailash. The Snow Goose rarely slept without Katherine by her side, but on this night she had stayed in her old nest, among the Snow Geese she hadn't seen in so very long. Kailash loved Katherine as much as he did. Kailash! Suddenly Nightlight had an idea that was both childish and knowing.

The children of Santoff Claussen huddled with Kailash in the nesting cave. The terrible news of Katherine's abduction had reached every corner of the Lamadary.

When Nightlight arrived at the cave, he found Tall William doing his best to appear brave and strong while Sascha and Petter readied a saddle. The children had decided to try and save Katherine themselves while riding Kailash. Nightlight knew better than to laugh or scold them for attempting this impossible mission.

He reached over to Kailash and gently stroked

her feathers. She gave a low, woeful honk, then rested her head on Nightlight's slender shoulder.

He knew his idea would work. He gathered the geese and the children together.

And so began a strange parade—Nightlight, followed by a dozen or so children and a flock of Giant Snow Geese, made their way through the Lamadary, past Yetis who were sharpening weapons in preparation for a great battle, past Lunar Lamas who were thumbing through their ancient books looking for clues that might help Katherine, and past the villagers from Santoff Claussen, who were standing about in worried clumps, sharing ideas and comforts. They didn't stop, not even to answer Old William's question about where they were going, until they reached Katherine's room.

They found Queen Toothiana there. Her back

was toward them—one of her iridescent wings dangled limply.

North was asking her in a gentle yet urgent voice, "And why in the world would Pitch come after you?"

Toothiana answered; her voice had a low cooing quality. "When I'd left the Monkey King, I flew up to Punjam Hy Loo. I found my mother's sisters, the Sisters of Flight. They had been waiting for me! But as they greeted me, they seemed so very sad. They asked of my mother. When I told them of her death, their leader sighed. 'We felt it, we thought it, now we know it to be true,' she told me." Toothiana's own eyes filled with tears, but she continued.

"The sisters formed a circle around the flying elephant, and one by one—right in front of me!—they turned into wood, like carved statues. Branches began to grow from them, branches that weaved themselves together like a giant basket. And as the last sister began to stiffen and change, she said to me, 'If one of us dies, we all die; you are queen here now. You must tend the elephant. He will protect all the memories of us, the memories of everything.'" Toothiana's one strong wing flapped ever more quickly.

"The elephant never forgets," Toothiana told them again. "It is he who touched the fabled Magic Tooth my parents bequeathed me. It is he who saw the memories that dwelled inside."

"But whose tooth is it?" asked Ombric in a hushed tone.

"The one who lives in the Moon," she answered.

The Lunar Lamas all murmured at once with excitement. "The tooth of the Man in the Moon!"

"Astounding!" said Ombric. "Toothiana has one of the five relics."

North needed to know more. "But what power does it bestow, Your Highness?"

"With it I can see the memories within the teeth. And once, when I was caged by this royal primate," she said, pointing her sword at the Monkey King, who was now bound by heavy shackles and chains, "I asked it to help me. It was then that I became more than I am. That is when there was more of me."

As if to explain better, the six mini-versions of Toothiana fluttered down from their perches in the candelabra that hung from the ceiling. They landed on Toothiana's shoulders, three on each side, and bowed.

Ombric pulled at his beard, thinking. This he had *never* seen. "Pitch could make much mischief if he were able to use that relic—maybe even harness the power of the flying elephant," he told them uneasily.

Nightlight felt a cold chill. Sascha, standing in the doorway beside him, couldn't help herself. She gasped, and Toothiana and the others spun around. The queen was even grander than the children had imagined. Her wings—they were magnificent—the most beautiful shades of blues and greens. Her eyes were as bright as a bird's, and her headdress was as glorious as any peacock's. And she was covered in a layer of tiny green and blue feathers that caught the light like prisms and filled the room with tiny reflected rainbows.

As the children stood, staring in awe, Kailash and one of the other Snow Geese stepped forward, honking. Kailash went on for quite some time. Toothiana's expression lit up when she learned that they could fix her wing, for she was, of course, fluent in all the bird languages, Snow Goose being a particular favorite.

Ombric placed a hand on North's arm. "Come, it's time to leave the queen to her helpers," he told him. "She's suffered a terrible injury and needs time to recover."

"We must rescue Katherine now!" said North. "Every second counts."

Bunnymund shook his head. He, too, was nearly desperate with worry about Katherine, but he would never let his emotions take over. Why, that would make him practically *human*. "I'll dig a tunnel to wherever we need to go, but first it would be most advantageous to know what to expect when we get there, and whether or not chocolate eggs will be required."

North had been in too many battles in his young life to ignore the sense in Bunnymund's words. He reluctantly agreed, but that didn't mean he was finished questioning the monkey. He grabbed him by the arm and dragged him toward the door, followed by Ombric and Bunnymund. "We'll be back," he called to Toothiana.

The Snow Geese, now cooing, began repairing the queen's damaged wing. Nightlight and the children stayed out of the way, watching the miraculous work of the geese. With unimaginable delicacy, they twined and smoothed each strand of Toothiana's crumpled feathers, layer after layer after layer. And slowly, the wing began to look as good as new.

The queen gave the injured wing a slight flutter. "Still hurts," she said, "but it is much better." Then she cocked her head from side to side, eyeing the children. "You should be asleep."

William the Absolute Youngest shook his head. "We're worried about our friend," he said.

Toothiana nodded, giving her repaired wing another careful flutter. She perched on the edge of Katherine's bed, turning her full attention to the children. Her very presence soothed them, just as it did the sleeping children she visited every night.

The youngest William now ventured a small smile. "We live in Santoff Claussen," he told her.

"It's the best village in the whole world," Sascha added. Then she gave a shiver. "Except for when the Nightmare King comes to visit."

The children began to tell Toothiana all about

their magical village and about the first time that Pitch's Fearlings had attacked them in the forest. "It was Katherine— She was the bravest, and she saved us," Tall William said.

"And that's when we first saw Nightlight!" his youngest brother added.

Petter, Fog, and the others acted out the various battles they'd seen.

Toothiana seemed properly impressed by their derring-do, and so the youngest William ventured to ask for a favor: "Can you—would you—make a wish on my next lost tooth? I don't have any loose ones right now, but you can pull one if you want." He opened his mouth as wide as he could so she could easily choose the best tooth.

"I needn't pull your tooth, but," Toothiana said, trying not to laugh, "name your wish."

"I wish for Katherine to come back to us, safe and sound," said William the Absolute Youngest.

"That's my wish too!" Sascha added.

"And mine," Petter said.

And one by one, the children asked for the same wish: the safe return of Katherine.

Toothiana listened carefully, then told them, "I will try."

Finally, William the Absolute Youngest—who may just have been William the *Wisest*—suggested they recite Ombric's first lesson.

And so, with Toothiana taking Katherine's place in their circle, the children joined hands and recited: "I believe. I believe. I believe."

But Nightlight did not join them. He stood alone. His face was blank and expressionless. Then full of fear.

North burst into the room, pressing through the door just ahead of Ombric and Bunnymund. "The monkey finally talked!" he said.

"We know his plan!" said Ombric.

"To Punjam Hy Loo?" Toothiana asked.

"And right speedily," replied Bunnymund.

Toothiana sprang to her feet, fluttered her wings, and brandished her swords. "Let's fly."

CHAPTER TWENTY-TWO

To Be Brave . . .

AN OMINOUS WIND BEGAN to blow in Punjam Hy Loo. Pitch looked down at Katherine. She was determined not to look surprised to see him.

"Thought I was done for, didn't you?" he asked in a voice icy with scorn. "No, my dear. It's your so-called Guardians who will be destroyed."

Katherine knew that the Nightmare King fed on fear—particularly the fear of children—and so she steeled herself to meet his cold, dark eyes with her own. She reminded herself of when last they'd met, when she'd held up the locket-size picture of his long-lost daughter. One look at it had made Pitch scream in agony. It had defeated him. Caused him and his Fearling army to vanish. And his scream had haunted Katherine ever since. She even felt a vague sort of pity for him. That pity gave her courage. And she was sure that Nightlight, North, and the others would soon fly to her rescue.

"The Guardians battled you in the Himalayas and at the center of the Earth," she said evenly, "and each time, *we* won the day."

Pitch's expression betrayed little. He slid closer to her, his dark cape covering so much of him that it was impossible to tell if he actually walked or if he floated. One thing was apparent: He kept his right hand, the hand that had become flesh, hidden under the cape, and his entire right side seemed stiff, as if underneath the cape he hid a terrible wound.

He stood perfectly still. Katherine looked to where his hand was hidden and wondered about the locket. Did he have it still?

Pitch sensed her thoughts. "You preyed on my weakness, and that was very clever." He brought his face close to hers. "But soon I'll be rid of any weakness. Your new Golden Age," he added, his voice becoming a calm whisper, "will become the Age of Nightmares!"

The monkeys began to screech in unison. They pounded their paws against the ancient blocks of stone they sat upon. One of them swung, paw over paw, down from the top of the ruins and landed in front of Pitch.

"Where is your king?" Pitch asked blankly. The monkey muttered a reply.

"Left behind?" said Pitch with a hint of

bemusement. "Betrayed by his own. All the better! Do you have the relic?"

The animal held up a pouch. From within this small sack there came a bright red glow, emanating from the ruby box snatched from Queen Toothiana!

Katherine recognized that glow—it was the same glow she'd seen coming from the orb of North's sword and on Bunnymund's egg-tipped staff . . . It was the glow of an ancient Lunar relic! She immediately averted her gaze, not wanting to arouse Pitch's suspicions as to the box's importance. But, she realized, this must be what gave Queen Toothiana whatever powers she possessed. Was this what Pitch was after?

Hoping to distract him, she blurted out, "You'll fail. You always do."

Pitch drew himself up, growing ever taller until he towered above her, and then he leaned over, his icy breath in her face. The air suddenly felt as cold as Siberia in winter.

Too late, Katherine realized her mistake. She had insulted Pitch's intelligence. Drat! She should have let him keep talking, let him talk all night, give her friends the time they needed to get to her.

"But what do I know," Katherine stammered, trying to placate him. "You're the Nightmare King and I'm just a girl."

Pitch permitted himself a small smile. "That's exactly right. The Man in the Moon's *toys* are of some use to me. But the prize I seek is of greater value—*much* greater. With it I can make an undefeatable army."

"What prize is that?" Katherine asked, using her sweetest, most innocent voice.

Pitch stared at her but said no more.

Katherine had to keep him talking, she had to! She had to trick him into revealing his plan—it was vital. She racked her brain for a compliment that he might believe, a compliment that would make him want to tell all—just so that he could boast.

"You've been brilliant at coming up with ways to thwart us—like sneaking into North's djinni or creating armor from the Earth's core," she said. "Why, I can't begin to imagine how astounding and dreadful this new prize will be."

Then she held her breath, waiting, while Pitch considered her words.

His eyes lit up. Katherine's heart pounded. *Pitch's need to boast would win out over his need for caution!*

She did not realize was that her lost tooth, which she held tightly in her hand, had begun to glow almost as brightly as the ruby-carved box.

Before she knew what had happened, the tooth was harshly snatched from her hand. A monkey soldier shuffled away from her, clutching the tooth. He tossed it to Pitch, who caught it easily with his left hand. He wrapped his fist around the tooth and pressed it against his forehead. His eyes closed, and he began to chuckle with diabolical glee. He was reading her tooth's memories!

"Stop, stop!" Katherine cried. "Those are *my* memories!" But a pair of monkeys sprang upon her, holding her tight, keeping her from attacking Pitch. His eyes stayed shut as if sleeping, and he saw every memory of hers he needed.

When at last he opened his hand again, the tooth was black and rotted.

It turned to dust and blew away in the wind.

Desperate, Katherine reached for the dust, but it

was gone. She sank to the ground. She felt so lost and alone. She began to clutch the compass around her neck. It was the first gift that North had ever given to her—a compass with an arrow that pointed to a single letter N, to North himself. Katherine had once used it to find North and Ombric in the Himalayas, and now—she was absolutely sure—it would show her that North was on his way to rescue her. Together they would put an end to this Nightmare Man.

But before she could look, Pitch crooked one of his long, black fingers, and the compass flew to him. His eyes still closed, he held the compass for a moment, then lobbed it at her feet.

"Your North isn't coming," he said, an edge of triumph in his voice. "The arrow isn't moving."

Pitch had learned enough of Ombric's magic to damage the compass. And now he also knew Katherine's most precious memories as well as many things about her and the Guardians. And he was quite sure he now knew how best to defeat them all.

Katherine grabbed the compass back. She stared at it in disbelief. The arrow spun uselessly, pointing nowhere. Why weren't North and the others on their way?

"They've abandoned you, their precious Katherine. To me." His voice turned smooth and cunning as he pretended to comfort her. "Your rightful place is at my side. Everyone's known that from the very moment you reminded me that I once had a daughter. I lost her, just like you lost your parents."

Katherine winced. "Don't," she cried. "Please, please don't!" Fighting back tears, she pressed North's compass to her heart. She closed her eyes and tried to recite Ombric's first spell: *I believe, I believe.* But doubts flooded her mind. She'd never recover her memories of her parents. She'd never know if they had loved her with the same fierce love that Pitch harbored for his daughter. An empty feeling filled her soul.

"You long for that, don't you?" he asked. "For the love of a parent—a father. I can give that to you. . . ." His voice was low, coaxing. "The locket—you know the one—it has your face in it now. You've seen it in your dreams, haven't you?"

Katherine shook as doubt and fear coursed through her. She *had* seen it. She'd *had* that nightmare—of being Pitch's daughter.

"You couldn't count on your parents," Pitch continued, his eyes once again glittering. "They left you.

When you were just a baby. What kind of parents do THAT? And your friends—your *Guardians*—why, you can see for yourself that they aren't coming." Pitch pointed to the compass again. The arrow still hadn't budged. "Without me, you'd be alone. Abandoned. Again."

Suddenly, Pitch swirled around. The monkeys, whose chant had been drumming quietly in the background, now began to screech.

With a ghoulish laugh, Pitch flew off, a trail of black smoke, into the night, leaving Katherine alone— more alone that she had ever been in her young life.

CHAPTER TWENTY-THREE

In Which the Guardians Fly to Punjam Hy Loo

BACK IN THE LUNAR Lamadary, North was filling Toothiana in on the best ways to battle Pitch. "If we surprise him, we will have an advantage," he told her.

Toothiana and her six mini-selves understood. They took to the sky. Nightlight started after her, then stopped, looking over his shoulder at the other Guardians. Toothiana made a trill-like noise and the mini-selves hovered in midflight, too.

"Go!" Bunnymund urged. "I'll tunnel the rest of us there."

"Pitch will be watching the skies," Ombric mused. "If we come from both air *and* underground, we may surprise him."

Queen Toothiana nodded sharply and set off toward Punjam Hy Loo, Nightlight on her heels and her six mini-selves flying just ahead.

The train was ready, filled with Yetis and Lunar Lamas and the villagers. If the Guardians were surprised to see the villagers already on the train, they didn't take the time to say so. Tall William, Fog, Petter, and all the children were aboard, as were North's elves. Bunnymund walked toward the front, North dragging the Monkey King after him. He shackled him to a door in the engine car.

"You might make a useful bargaining chip, Your Royal *Monkeyness*," North growled. "Just don't cause any trouble."

North and Ombric stood at the controls in the front car as Bunnymund readied himself near the tip of the digging device. "Let's get going, Bunnymund!" North urged. "We've got to *move*!"

Bunnymund turned to his friends. He held a particularly large chocolate egg in one paw. "It's time again to unleash the inner Pooka," he said with a flourish. Then he swallowed the chocolate whole.

North grimaced. "Oh, boy. I'm never sure what's going to happen when he goes nutty with the chocolate."

"He told me that once he grew an extra head," Ombric offered cheerfully.

And indeed, Bunnymund began to twist and grow and change with alarming suddenness, and before they could tell if he'd grown anything extra, he became a giant blur of digging. Even for a Pooka, he was moving astonishingly fast. All they could see in front of them was a blizzard of dirt and rocks.

At the same time, Ombric's beard and eyebrows began to twirl. He was finally sensing bits of thoughts from Katherine, and he was most concerned. The thoughts that made it through to him were full of despair. North sensed this too, but he had more immediate concerns.

"We've never had a crazier plan," he confided to Ombric.

"Nicholas, we have what we need. Brave hearts. And sharp minds," Ombric reminded him. "And as you might recall, we always abandon our plans and end up doing things we never imagined."

North smiled. The old man still had a thing or two to teach him.

CHAPTER TWENTY-FOUR

Anger, Despair, and a Wisp of Hope

KATHERINE HUGGED HER KNEES to her chest and tried to quell the feeling of hopelessness that was starting to overwhelm her. Sweat formed on her temples and on her upper lip. She felt as if disaster was closing in, and indeed it was. The monkeys dropped down from the ruined walls and formed a circle around her.

She tried to block out their howling, but it grew louder and more insistent as the animals came closer. Her heart seemed to be beating to the rhythm of their chant.

Where are my friends? They have to know where I am by now! She gazed at the compass and its motionless arrow: North was not on his way to rescue her. And her tooth—its memories were lost forever.

She'd never felt such rage.

Katherine got to her feet and glared at the monkeys. They were spinning faster and faster in a circle around her, chanting louder and louder. She covered her ears and screamed, "Stop it! Stop it!"

But the monkeys' grins only widened. And then they resumed their shrieking chant.

Katherine sank to her knees, gripping the compass in her hands. She didn't know what to do. *Where is North? Where is Nightlight? How can they not have come to get me?* And the despair overtook the anger, overtook the outrage, overtook reason.

Why did my parents die when I was too young to remember them?!

Maybe it would be easier to give up, she thought. To go along with Pitch and become his Darkling Daughter. At least this terrible pain would go away. She looked up at the sky and tried to make out the Man in the Moon's face. But swirling clouds blocked him out. It was as if even the Man in the Moon had turned his back on her.

Ignoring the monkeys, Katherine began to scratch at the ground with her fingers; the dirt was soft, and soon she'd made a small hole. She paused for a moment, then dropped the compass in. She pressed dirt over it. Then she curled up and lay upon the small mound.

I'm tired of fighting, she thought. *I don't want to grow up.*

A breeze stirred the air, and Katherine was glad for at least that, at least a moment of coolness. And that's when she saw, in the distance, what appeared to be a hummingbird making its way toward her.

CHAPTER TWENTY-FIVE

A Brief Exchange as the Watchful Are Watched

As NIGHTLIGHT AND TOOTHIANA flew toward Punjam Hy Loo, the wind and clouds seemed to be moving with them. For the second time in as many days, Nightlight had the feeling he was being watched. Toothiana, he noticed, was glancing about from side to side, as if she felt the same. Nightlight tried to see if Toothiana could hear his thoughts. *Are you having this "watching" feeling?* he asked her in thought.

For a moment she did not respond, but just when he'd decided she didn't share the same gift he and the Guardians did, she turned her head in her sudden, birdlike way and looked him in the eye, her glorious wings never missing a beat. "I do, Quiet Boy," she said above the wind. "I've felt 'the watching' many times. She is a mystery. But she is always there. In the wind. The rain. The snow. The thunder and the lightning. I do not know if she is bad or good. But what interest she has in the battle to come? I cannot say."

CHAPTER TWENTY-SIX

The Reckoning

THERE WAS A STRANGE moment as they approached Punjam Hy Loo. Every Guardian felt it, including Toothiana. They no longer wanted to merely defeat Pitch or imprison him or send him into exile. They wanted him to die.

Because of rage or sorrow or hate or revenge or even cold, calculated logic, they wanted to kill him. It was a dark reckoning. Each of them looked for the Moon, hoping that their friend and leader would tell them what to do. But a storm had blackened the skies.

And they were on their own.

CHAPTER TWENTY-SEVEN

Can a Pooka Grow Six Arms?

THE JOURNEY WAS EXTREMELY swift; the first car of the egg-shaped train popped quietly above the earth near the peak of Punjam Hy Loo. North unshackled the Monkey King, grasped him by the neck, and dragged him out. The Cossack's sword was aglow. Ombric climbed out right behind him.

Bunnymund motioned for them to be quiet. And quiet they were. Dumbfounded, actually. For Bunnymund was a hulking mess, covered with layers of mud and pulverized rock dust that made him look more like a statue than a giant rabbit. His cloak was gone, torn to nothingness. But what was most surprising—the chocolate he'd eaten had turned him into a massive, muscular warrior version of himself, and as an extra little surprise, he now had six arms, three on each side.

North frowned. "This is too odd, even for me."

"Oh, don't worry," replied Bunnymund cheerfully. "I'll go back to being bi-armed when we're done." Then he shushed North with all three right hands. North thought the gesture pointless—how could they be heard above the strange chanting that echoed through the dense jungle?

They looked around. The darkness was nearly total. Not a star shined through what seemed to him ominous-looking clouds, and the wind seemed to be blowing in gusts from every direction. Toothiana and Nightlight flew down from the topmost

Bunnymund ate the six-armed chocolate again!

branches of a huge banyan tree to join them.

"Just ahead. In a clearing," Toothiana said quietly. "Katherine."

"Any Fearlings?" asked North.

Toothiana shook her head. "Monkeys. An army of monkeys."

"Our relics won't have the same effect on creatures of flesh and blood," said Ombric, worried.

"Pitch is most cunning," said Toothiana.

"Indeed," replied North. "But we can handle them."

"The monkeys are a dangerous mix," she cautioned. "Part man. Part animal. The worst parts of each. And they obey no law, not even the jungle's. They are an army to be feared."

"My army!" the Monkey King screeched.

"Silence!" North hissed. He threw him to his elves. "Guard him," he ordered. Then, tossing aside his overcoat and using the glowing orb on his sword to light the way, he stormed through the thick, steamy jungle toward the chanting primates.

The wind picked up and swirled around them. Toothiana knew the way so she sped ahead of North to lead them through the vines. They pushed past immense tropical plants and webs of vines for what seemed an eternity, until the chanting suddenly stopped.

The Guardians could tell they were edging into the clearing now; the jungle seemed less dense, and they could just make out the shapes of structures and buildings ahead. North's saber grew brighter, as did the egg at the tip of Bunnymund's staff. But Nightlight kept dim. To do what he had planned, he needed to be stealthy.

The relics provided enough light for them to see

the monkey army that had gathered along every stone, pile, and tower that filled the city of Punjam Hy Loo. Toothiana flared her wings and hissed at them. "We are just outside the Temple of the Flying Elephant," she whispered.

The Guardians pressed forward until they came to a wall of monkeys. The Guardians drew their weapons, expecting to be set upon, but to their surprise, the creatures shuffled aside to let them pass. They were armed with all sorts of weapons: daggers, swords, spears, and each was crudely armored.

Bunnymund's whiskers twitched. "Pitch is quite resourceful in his choice of henchmen. Or should I say henchmonkeys?"

North was unimpressed. His sword would make quick work of these monkey boys.

With a nod from Toothiana, Nightlight darted

past the others and disappeared into the dark. As the others moved past the last layer of monkeys, they could see a single torch shining in the dark just ahead, its flame being battered by the winds. Then they spied Katherine, bound by thick vines and lashed to a post in front of the giant doors of the flying elephant's temple. Behind her stood Pitch. Around his neck hung Toothiana's ruby box.

"One step more," warned Pitch, bringing one of his long, black fingers to within a hairbreadth of Katherine's cheek, "and I make her *mine*."

They stopped. The wind picked up. A spider's web of lightning lit the sky.

Pitch smiled a sly smile and then roared a command.

The monkey army launched its attack.

CHAPTER TWENTY-EIGHT

A Monkey Battle Royale

THE MONKEYS ATTACKED WITH a fury that surprised even North. The hilt of his sword wrapped itself tightly around his hand, and he slashed at the screaming creatures they descended upon them.

"Do your magic, old man!" North shouted to Ombric, hoping the wizard had a spell or two that would help combat this onslaught. North swung left and right, but he missed his mark more often than he wished. *With humans,* he thought, *you can anticipate what they'll do, but these monkeys are insane.*

Toothiana flew above the fray, expertly wielding

Ready to attack!

her swords, bucking and spinning whenever a monkey landed on her back, trying to rip at her wings.

Bunnymund was able to do considerable damage to any simian within reach of his six massive arms.

All the while, Nightlight was creeping quietly along the top of the temple, staying in the shadows. And with him? Toothiana's six tiny selves. They were waiting for their moment.

The timbre of the monkeys' screeches was deafening. And for every monkey the Guardians felled, three more seemed to arrive to take its place. They swooped down from the treetops like giant locusts. Their swarms made it nearly impossible to get closer to Katherine. And the heat, the dastardly heat! Sweat poured from his brow; North could hardly see.

And so he was unaware of the villagers and the Yetis and his elf men, dragging the pitiful Monkey

King with them, joining in the fight. Even the boys—
Petter, Fog, and Tall William—grabbed on to thick
vines and swung into the middle of the action, sport-
ing Yeti-crafted daggers. "Free me!" the bedraggled
king cried out, but his army paid him no mind; they
followed Pitch now.

Ombric, for his part, was doing his best to calm
the unnerving wind. At one moment it seemed to
favor Pitch and the monkeys, pushing North back as
he neared Katherine, but in the next, a blast of air
sent a monkey's arrow into the trunk of a banyan
tree instead of into North's forehead. Even the huge
Yetis fought to make headway against the hurricane-
force gales. But despite trying all his meteorological
enchantments, Ombric failed to still the eerie gusts
that coiled and twisted about the combatants.

And even with all their manpower, even with all

of their weapons, and even with all of Ombric's wizarding capabilities, the Guardians could not keep up with the monkey horde. It was as if Pitch had called every monkey in the world into his service.

Pitch stood back and surveyed the scene with satisfaction. He taunted Guardians and monkeys alike, enjoying the chaos he caused.

"Bravo!" he cheered as a monkey catapulted itself toward Toothiana's back. Then he laughed out loud when Toothiana dodged the flying creature and it plummeted to the ground in a broken heap.

He smiled with gruesome delight as a trio of monkeys waged a game of catch with Gregor of the Mighty Smile and Sergei the Giggler. They tossed the pair about like toys while the other elves tried to rescue their hapless friends.

The Guardians themselves were beginning to

stagger with exhaustion. North found he was missing more than he was hitting—never had he found himself in such a situation. Even Bunnymund could barely lift any of his six arms to fight off the endless, screeching horde. At last Ombric raised up his staff and called out frantically, "Enough! Enough! We are beaten, Pitch!"

"Never!" North immediately contested. But he, too, was incapable of continuing—if his relic sword had not been attached to his hand, he would surely have dropped it.

The monkeys encircled them and readied for the kill.

Pitch was delighted. This was exactly what he wanted: for the Guardians and all who followed them to feel defeated.

He raised his dark hand, and the monkeys froze.

They did, however, keep their weapons poised.

The Guardians and Toothiana stumbled forward, panting. Bunnymund had to hold up North with one set of arms and Ombric with the other.

"What is it you seek, Pitch?" Ombric asked, gasping.

"The flying elephant," he said simply.

Toothiana's eyes narrowed. "He will do only as I command," she told Pitch.

"Oh, I know that, *Your Highness*. Please remind me—what is it you are queen of? Ah yes, a bunch of ruins. A handful of little fairies and a flying elephant. An elephant that no one *ever* sees. Not much of a kingdom."

Queen Toothiana spread her wings and hissed at Pitch.

"Most articulate, Your Highness. Now, BRING

OUT THE ELEPHANT, or I'll take this child"—
Pitch placed his hand dangerously close to Katherine's
brow—"and blacken her soul forever."

Toothiana took a step toward Pitch, her swords
still ready. Her face was set; she seemed determined
to attack.

He gave her a shriveling look. "Oh, my dear girl.
Your dinner knives can't harm me."

At that moment the Monkey King wrenched himself away from his elf captors and hobbled quickly to
Pitch. "Master!" he blubbered. "You'll make the elephant give me back my humanity?"

Pitch looked down at the pitiful creature and
laughed. "No, you fool. I'll ask him to remove *all* of
mine."

The monkey looked almost comically confused.

"It's my only imperfection," Pitch went on. "I can

feel things. *Human* things. It's my only weakness." He glared at Toothiana. "You should understand that, Your Highness, being half human yourself. Think of what you might accomplish if *you* didn't have that burden."

Toothiana just stared at him.

"If the elephant can take away all of this miserable creature's weaknesses," he said, pointing to the monkey, "then it can surely take away mine."

"If that is what you wish," Toothiana said evenly.

"It's the only way you'll get her back," said Pitch, motioning to Katherine.

North, his face a storm of fury, called out, "He'll become invulnerable!"

Toothiana refused to look at North. "I cannot let harm come to any child."

Then she lowered her weapons and closed her

eyes. "Sisters of Flight, forgive me," she whispered. The Guardians gazed up at the wooden statues that ringed the base of the temple. They were magnificent effigies. Beautiful winged women standing straight and tall, but frozen forever.

"If only they could help," moaned Ombric. The wind calmed somewhat as the massive doors of the temple creaked slowly open.

At first they could see only darkness in the temple. Then the shuffle of heavy footsteps shook the ground.

CHAPTER TWENTY-NINE

The Dark Surprise
Or
All Is Given for the Sake of Pity

IT WAS TIME. THE trap was sprung. Everyone knew their part. The flying elephant exploded from its temple. Wings outstretched, trunk and tusks raised, it knocked Pitch away from Katherine and pinned him to the ground. At that exact moment Toothiana leaped to Katherine and, with one slash of her blade, cut the vines that bound her to the post. Her six mini-selves flew like darts from their hiding places atop the temple and yanked Toothiana's ruby-carved box from Pitch's neck. The monkey army, momentarily stunned by the surprise attack, quickly recovered and fell upon the Guardians, certain that they would kill them on the spot.

They were in for another surprise.

"No more playacting!" North shouted out, brandishing his swords with characteristic fury. Bunnymund and Ombric dropped their exhausted posing and became dervishes of action, knocking out monkeys by the score. The Yetis, elves, and citizens of Santoff Claussen followed suit. It had all been an act! They weren't beaten at all! The battle became feverish within seconds.

But there were more surprises yet.

Toothiana grabbed her ruby relic from her mini-selves, held it to her chest, and repeated the call she'd made only once before: "Mother, Father, help me." No sooner had she spoken these words than hundreds—no, thousands—of mini-versions of herself

Nicholas St. North will do his best against the worst.

began to stream from her like waves of light.

They swarmed the monkeys like an endless army of hornets, their tiny swords and arrows slicing the monkeys to ribbons.

Pitch struggled against the elephant's weight, and from the roof of the temple, Nightlight took careful aim. The final blow would come from his staff.

Katherine knew what was coming. One of Toothiana's mini-selves who had flown to her outside the temple had told her every detail of the Guardians' bold plan. Now that Katherine was free from Pitch's clutches, he would die. In a moment Nightlight's diamond-tipped staff, sharper than any spear—and the only weapon that had ever pierced the villain's heart—would do so once more.

All around was the crazy havoc of battle. Monkeys, Yetis, wizard, villains, and heroes were locked in a battle to the death. Everyone but Katherine. She stood still, looking down at Pitch. In that moment he knew her thoughts. He knew that his doom was an instant away. And Katherine saw fear in his eyes.

There was one thing she must know before the end. So she did something that was not in the plan.

CHAPTER THIRTY

The Winds of Change

NIGHTLIGHT BLINKED. HE COULDN'T throw his staff. Katherine was in the way!

Move! he thought as hard as he could. But Katherine did not answer.

He knew that something was terribly wrong. As fast as his considerable powers would propel him, he flew. But the disaster unfolded faster than could be reckoned with.

Katherine stared at Pitch's hand. Its flesh color had spread up his arm, all the way to the shoulder. But that's not what held her mesmerized. It was the locket. In his hand, Pitch still gripped the locket. In fact, the locket seemed to have fused to his fingers, become a part of him. The same locket that she had shown him at the battle of the Earth's core. The locket that had carried a picture of Pitch's lost daughter. But whose picture would be in it? Would Katherine's face be there? Would her nightmare be true?

It took all her courage to look. And then she saw. The picture was almost gone; only scraps of it remained—Pitch had clearly tried to tear it away. But Katherine could see just enough to know that it was the old image of Pitch's daughter. She felt a sort of relief, but then she looked in Pitch's eyes again. They were so anguished, afraid, lost in pain. *He doesn't deserve to die,* she thought. *Even the worst villain needs pity. He was a father and a hero once. He did not chart his past or the present.*

Pitch is fallen.

What Katherine felt, that strange mix of revulsion and sorrow that overwhelmed her, was instantly felt by all the Guardians.

Then Pitch's other hand reached out and grabbed hers. Her eyes widened. Pitch's touch was unexpectedly gentle.

Nightlight tried to break Pitch's hold on Katherine, but before he could do so, the wind picked up again, gusts of it whipping through the clearing, bending trees in half, ripping leaves from their branches.

The sky darkened faster than any of them ever experienced before. A swirling mass of clouds broke through the treetops and descended into the clearing. In the midst of it all was a tall, cloaked woman who held herself with a regal air. Her face was long yet lovely, and years older than they remembered from the picture they had seen. Icy nuggets of hail

*Mother Nature makes
a dramatic and unexpected appearance.*

and bolts of lightning churned around her as the cloud mass moved toward Pitch and Katherine, then engulfed them.

Then, as suddenly as the cloud had arrived, it was gone.

And with it, Katherine and Pitch.

The monkey army had scrambled back to the jungle. All who remained stood there speechless. Katherine was gone! They'd failed.

North was the first gather his wits. "That woman in the clouds. Pitch's daughter?"

Ombric looked at Nightlight. He did not have to ask the question out loud for Nightlight to understand.

Nightlight shimmered a response.

But his answer was one that Ombric never expected. He turned to Toothiana. She nodded. The old wizard blinked rapidly, processing what he'd just learned. North cleared his throat impatiently. "Spit it out, old man."

Ombric tugged at his beard once, then a second time, then at last he said, "She has another name, apparently. By some she's known as Mother Nature."

Bunnymund's left ear twitched, then his right one did same. "I've encountered this being before," said the Pooka. "She's not always a benevolent soul, and she is very unpredictable."

The villagers, the children, the Yeti—all of them gathered. The Guardians looked to the coming dawn, bound by one emotion. Not fear or hate or vengeance. It was that feeling of pity Katherine had for Pitch.

Toothiana spoke what everyone was feeling. "We didn't fail, but we did lose our way. We wanted to kill," she said softly.

"We were no better than Pitch. Perhaps worse," said Ombric.

"But Katherine remembered," said North quietly.

So they stood on the peak of Punjam Hy Loo, weary but alive and certain of one thing: Katherine's strength had been greater than theirs. And they hoped and believed that this strength would keep her safe past the dawn of this new day.

TO BE CONTINUED . . .

THE
SANDMAN
— ·◊· —
AND THE WAR OF DREAMS

*Featuring the desperate mission to save Katherine
and the appearance of a wayward lad of considerable
interest named Jackson Overland Frost.*

Also by William Joyce

THE GUARDIANS: BOOK ONE
Nicholas St. North and the Battle of the Nightmare King

THE GUARDIANS: BOOK TWO
E. Aster Bunnymund and the Warrior Eggs at the Earth's Core!

THE GUARDIANS OF CHILDHOOD: BOOK ONE
The Man in the Moon

THE GUARDIANS OF CHILDHOOD: BOOK TWO
The Sandman: The Story of Sanderson Mansnoozie